T0278286

The Lockmaster

THE GERMAN LIST

CHRISTOPH RANSMAYR

The Lockmaster

A Short Story of Killing

TRANSLATED BY SIMON PARE

LONDON NEW YORK CALCUTTA

This publication has been supported by a
grant from the Goethe-Institut India.

Seagull Books, 2024

Originally published as *Der Fallmeister. Eine kurze Geschichte vom Töten*
© S. Fischer Verlag GmbH, Frankfurt am Main, 2021

First published in English translation by Seagull Books, 2024
English translation © Simon Pare, 2024

ISBN 978 1 80309 370 3

British Library Cataloguing-in-Publication Data
A catalogue record for this book is available from the British Library.

Typeset by Seagull Books, Calcutta, India
Printed and bound in the USA by Integrated Books International

CONTENTS

ONE

The Great Falls

My father killed five people. Like most murderers who need only to press a key or push a lever or a switch to elevate themselves for one unfettered instant to the rank of masters of life and death, he did this without touching a hair on his victims' heads or even looking them in the eye but by means of a series of chrome winches to flood a navigation channel used by riverboats.

The surge of water released by the open sluice gates transformed this narrow channel lined with larch beams into a raging culvert. Instead of gliding gently through it from the upper to the lower reaches of the White River, a languid narrowboat with 12 people on board suddenly gathered speed and shot downstream between moss-covered cliffs. Then, where the passage rejoined the old river-bed, the longboat flipped over in the torrent, as if struck by a giant fist, and tumbled bottom-up through the seething whirlpools and currents.

The roar of the Great Falls, a cascade over 120 feet high which boats were able to bypass via a system of canals my father had regulated—no, ruled over—for almost 30 years, drowned out the horrified shrieks of those gathered on the craggy banks who witnessed the sinking as well as heard the screams and cries for help of the capsized and drowning passengers. All sound not produced by the eddies or the spray or the echo of the whitewater pounding against the rocks was swallowed up by the White River and its falls, a centuries-old source of dread to rafters and watermen.

It was a warm and slightly cloudy early summer's day, a Friday in May on which, according to a *Calendar of the Martyrs* observed both then and now, many villages and towns on the banks of the almost 2,000-mile-long river celebrated the feast of St Nepomuk— the patron saint of rafters, bridge-builders and lockkeepers, but above all the custodian of secrets. According to one legend carved in hand-sized gilded letters into a rock beside the Great Falls, Nepomuk, the bishop and imperial confessor of Prague, had refused to divulge a crime an emperor had avowed to him and had, as a result, been tortured and thrown into the swollen Vltava with a grindstone around his neck.

Even though by the time of his feast most ferry connections were already discontinued and many bridges that had once spanned the White River on its way to the Black Sea had been destroyed, the spirit of the bridge protector seemed to hover over dynamited and flooded pillars and shattered steel arches, over remains corroded by rust or crumbling under blankets of moss, smothered by deep-green thickets in the summer months, while in winter they loomed cold and black from the clouds of spray like the ghosts of a world that had sunk into infamy.

Over 40 languages were spoken along the White River, yet the number of bridges that had once stitched its banks together dwindled with every passing year, a clear and dramatic symbol of an age of division and borders. The loss of the bridges had been accompanied by the dissolution of most alliances and ties between states on the European continent, splintering it into a plethora of microstates, tiny principalities, counties and tribal territories, each boasting its own flag and coat of arms. The White River flowed as calmly and inexorably as ever towards a future in which only the occasional rotten barge or cable ferry would ply its way through the gurgling, frothing eddies that licked the rubble jutting from its waters.

Five dead. Whether my father had actually intended to cause so many casualties or a comparably alarming number—or was perhaps even willing to countenance the death of all twelve of the longboat's passengers—will presumably remain a mystery unless a confession nailed to the sluice gate or some other scrap of evidence turns up among the driftwood and jetsam along the gravel banks to confirm or refute my suspicions. Any question to him is but an echo in the void. On the first anniversary of his deed, as if after precisely one year's penance he had resolved to atone, he glided along the upper reaches of the White River past a shocked fly-fisherman who shouted a warning as the rock-salt-laden lighter, similar to the narrowboat in which my father's victims had capsized, headed for the veils of spray of the Great Falls.

He didn't even glance at the frantically gesticulating angler nor, according to the man's statement, take a single stroke with his oars to avert the inevitable. And with his cargo, he plunged into the thundering depths.

Smashed planks from his lighter were found on three different sandbanks and gravel shoals; his corpse—despite the deployment of rescue divers, who had never retrieved anything but dead bodies along this stretch of river—never was. And too much time has now passed to find in the deep, or hidden under an overgrown patch of riverbank, even one shard of bone that might be traced back to the missing man.

The rock salt he was transporting must also, I imagine, have wiped out schools of freshwater fish—rainbow trout, pike and char, which beat their fins so frenetically in their panicked escape from the gill-corroding salt dissolved in the swirling currents that they squandered what strength they had left and re-enacted how my father's victims met their watery deaths.

Shaped like a Venetian gondola, the nearly 30-foot larchwood punt in which my father vanished silently into the Great Falls, like a boatman petrified by guilt, was drawn from the stocks of the open-air museum of river navigation that he had run for decades with an unquenchable hatred for all things modern. After all, if one thing could be said with any certainty about my father—an enthusiastic and sometimes kindly man whose silences could last for days and who had frequent outbursts of rage—it was that he was a man of the past, not only as the administrator of an extensive museum complex but also to the very core of his being.

By the time he was appointed lockmaster and thus curator of the Great Falls Museum in our home county of Bandon, the course of his life seemed to have changed direction, and rather than flowing into a forbidding future, ran backwards out of the fog of this future into a yesteryear that appeared familiar, predictable and amenable.

Centuries earlier, in times that lived on only in my father's mind, *lockmaster* had been an honorific title granted to the lockkeepers who diverted the White River around the Great Falls into boat channels built like watery terraces along the cliffs. These had allowed the salt skippers to skirt the Great Falls in their lighters via a series of stepped canals.

His job was to let just the right amount of water into these passages by opening and closing a series of sluice gates, so that even heavily laden salt punts could be carried past the roaring falls and into the lower reaches of the White River on a gentle wave whose force decreased with every yard. Thus, by the end of the deviation, the surge of water would have been sapped by the staggered opening of drain valves and, slowed only by wet larchwood boards, a lighter would slide gently back out onto the river.

A lockmaster exerted such masterly control of the sequential opening and closing of the sluice gates, the valves, the flooding and the discharge, that the boatmen in their descending lighters floated around the Great Falls as if in a cradle or the basket of a hot-air balloon. But woe betide him if he made even one mistake during this descent! A longboat could shoot downstream like a harpoon tip before capsizing and sinking into the whitewater at the end of its passage. The dozens of sailors who had drowned over the centuries of this salt trade were commemorated on plaques screwed into a bare rockface beside the Great Falls or carved, like the legend of St Nepomuk's drowning, into the stone as intricate ornaments, now coated with moss.

Although the age of the lockmasters was long gone, although the mouths of the salt mines in the Totengebirge mountains, whose towering, cloud-scraping walls bounded the county's southern horizon, were now scrub-choked or blocked-up portals, and the boat passages overhanging the river mere artefacts to be admired for a modest entry fee, although he was the curator, my father stubbornly insisted on being addressed as *lockmaster*.

Shortly before the latest ethnic laws forced my mother Jana to leave him and return to her native Adriatic shores, she embroidered the chest pocket of one of his shirts, where he always kept the river-flow chart handy, with his title in silver thread: *Lockmaster*. I now know that even without this ethnic cleansing, Jana would probably have left my father because she could no longer stand Bandon's universal hatred of all things foreign nor my father's hatred for every aspect of contemporary life.

Lockmaster! To me and my sister Mira, who had overheard local people make sarcastic jibes and giggle about the curator's self-appointed title, it seemed at the time as if, before her departing, our mother had embroidered a mocking nickname on his chest, and he took it with him to his doom.

According to his sometimes conspiratorial-sounding stories, he had become curator of the Great Falls Museum purely by vocation—after all, he said, the highlight of every single day of his childhood had been his mother telling him a river legend that repeatedly transported him back into a nameless past. Her tales of river spirits, kelp forests, water sprites and floating, shape-shifting denizens of the dark riverbed, her tales of the depths and of high water had apparently lulled him to sleep each evening.

His mother, a so-called *water burgess*, had given public lectures and visited schools to pass on the stories she had herself once been told. When she died on the brink of her 100th birthday, my father had urged his wife, Jana, to sustain these evocations of the water-world deep into my sister Mira's childhood years and mine too. My mother would really much rather have told us about her coastline, the islands of the Adriatic and mermaids rather than about river spirits, but she was forbidden from doing so.

On every anniversary of my grandmother's death, my parents, Mira and I would stand with bouquets of blue lilies at her graveside in the section of Bandon cemetery known as *Lockmaster Heaven*, and stare, as we half mumbled and half sang prayers and invocations, at the four words my father had had carved into the gravestone:

Once upon a time.

I first heard about the St Nepomuk's Day disaster during a video call with Mira that was interrupted by screen blackouts and the crackle of interference. At the time I was working as a hydraulic engineer in Brazil on various dams across the Rio Xingu, a tributary of the Amazon, and I heard the news about Bandon, usually with a few days' delay, from my sister via an unstable internet connection that could only really be relied on during the stiflingly hot nights.

In my months there, the Kayapó, a forest people living on the banks of the Rio Xingu, were waging a desperate war with arrows, spears and axes against a dam that would drown their entire world—their villages, hunting grounds and sacred sites. It was only when I visited the building lots scattered around the tropical wilderness that I realized that my work was contributing to this apocalypse. The first time I heard of the Kayapó indios was two weeks after my arrival, when they destroyed the satellite receivers and glass-fibre cables of the electricity company laying the ground-work for the impending deluge. From that point on, my assigned surveying team, which was responsible for installing the penstocks, only left the camp with a trigger-ready guard of Brazilian army pioneers.

Mira was disappointed, angry in fact, that even after the news of our father's disappearance, I could not leave my Amazonian construction site to be with her and help her clear the lockmaster's house by the Great Falls. Not once had our mother Jana mentioned this house since her departure, neither in her electronic mail nor in her video conversations with Mira, and according to a message she sent only to my sister, she was now living on the Adriatic island of Cres with a *water warrior* who fought at monthly intervals as a mercenary on dammed sections of the River Jordan. She had no desire to go along on the final journey of a husband chained to the past, whom she had long loved in vain and eventually come to hate. Then, as now, she was unaware that this man was not merely obsessed with the past but was also a murderer.

Five dead!

Among the drowned on that fateful day in May was a turbine attendant at Hydroelectric Plant IV on the White River, who left behind a Baghdad-born wife and two children.

Drowned was a seamstress whose deaf daughter let out guttural gasps as she attempted to climb into the open grave at her mother's funeral, and had to be forcibly restrained by the gravedigger who had fled from civil war.

Drowned was a retired farm mechanic, as well as a builder of wooden boats and an amateur astronomer who tried, on clear nights, to capture signals of intelligent life from the depths of space.

Drowned was the trombonist from a brass band who had belted out the 'Rafters' Hymn' against the roar of the rapids from the garlanded lighter before it cast off.

Also drowned was a childless music teacher with alopecia areata whose tumbledown half-timbered house was surrounded by a field of strawberries. The house was just far enough from the banks of the White River that only a dull thundering from the Great Falls was audible in its sunlit rooms. Nevertheless, a column of spray, towering high above the riparian forest and veiled with occasional rainbows, filled its west-facing windows during snowmelt season and deep into the summer.

The turbine attendant from The Falls Hydroelectric Plant IV, not 2 miles from my hometown of Bandon, was 43 years old when he drowned on St Nepomuk's Day. The seamstress was 56; the music teacher, whom the strawberry pickers called the *catwoman* on account of the dozens of stray cats she fed daily, was 37.

Their pike-nibbled corpses were only recovered five, eight and nine weeks respectively after the apparent accident. This was because the White River, through whose foaming rapids the drowners had tumbled after the garlanded lighter capsized, thunders for over 60 miles through Bandon county in a tangle of gorges riven with distributaries, fjord-like bays and vortex streets. Even on my simulation software, the flow ratios indicate utter havoc.

All my father's victims had lived, if not within sight, then at least within earshot of the Great Falls. Its thunderous noise had formed the acoustic backdrop of my childhood and youth too, and even during my years working on dams across the great rivers of Africa, South America and Asia, I often yearned for the bewitching, deep-green beauty of those legend-laden, myth-charged playgrounds along the sandbanks and gravel shoals of the White River's gorges.

Dragonflies of every colour and size hung there against a summer sky bordered by the edges of a ravine, as if the glittering water had transfixed and transported them into a buzzing serenity they could only achieve by hovering. Kingfishers sat motionlessly, like tree decorations, on their hunting perches before darting out of their torpor—as if some detonation had exploded deep within their sparkling blue plumage—and dropping on a tiny translucent fish lying wait for its own prey just below the surface.

Back then, I saw hunting kingfishers as magical manifestations of the ineluctable nature of killing and being killed. I paid with repeated fever and severe colds for spending long periods—sometimes hours!—submerged up to the crown of my head inside a kingfisher's territory, equipped only with snorkel and diving mask, waiting for the hunter to detach itself from its perch and the sky blue beyond and swoop down on its victim in the watery depths, cloaked in a cloud of silvery bubbles. For years I waited for this moment in vain.

It took me a long time to realize how much I resembled my father in my memories and in my yearning for these riparian forests and riverbanks; he had never wanted to leave the shadow of the mists that swirled above the Great Falls even in the summer months, never wanted to leave the gorges that *his* river had carved over the millennia into the limestone mountains visible from Bandon.

As a hireling of various water armies, I had tried to create the conditions for converting current into energy on the Zambezi and the White Nile and around the sources of the Paraná, the Okavango, the Niger, the Euphrates, the Rio Xingu and the Mekong—and it had only started to dawn on me in the first days after the news of the disaster at the Great Falls that I might in fact, after my own fashion, be just as incapable of leaving behind the White River as my father had been.

When, as a child, I was allowed to accompany him through seething spray on one of his control trips in a lighter powered by an outboard motor or on his walks along a system of soaring, gorge-spanning rope bridges that led us to sluice systems, disintegrating towpaths, groynes, flooded relief channels and rotting wooden breakwaters, we sometimes moulded colluvial deposits on the river-banks into figures whose sun-baked remnants were visible through-out the summer and sometimes until the first snow fell.

According to my father, we were, like any omnipotent being, *creating* realistically sized dogs, rats and cats from the grey clay, and once even an almost life-sized man crouching on a water-lapped rock, which river-goers paddling past in their kayaks or canoes initially mistook for a fisherman and, each time they passed after that, bombarded it with pebbles taken from the shallow bot-tom passing beneath their boats until it was gone. Yet to this day I can tell the exact spot on the rock where our creation, our Adam, sat with his hazel-switch fishing rod and confounded those paddlers.

In the springtime, one ledge of this rock was clad with primroses and deep-blue gentian, of which my father would always pick one blossom, never more, for my mother, who cherished blue wild-flowers more than any other, because blue was the colour of the sea on happy days, the colour of *her* Adriatic, whose rocky coastline she had fled as a girl during one of the endless Dalmatian wars.

One other thing that repeatedly pops into my memory are the gardens of Bandon and, seemingly in the midst of them, the catwoman's strawberry beds—long rows, protected by wood wool from winter frosts, where all the inhabitants of Bandon were allowed to pick as much as they wanted in the early summer. During the harvest, the windows of the half-timbered house would remain open, and through them would come the sound of the catwoman singing. And while the bent-backed berry pickers scoured the beds for the sweetest and largest fruits and secretly chortled at her rippling coloraturas, she sat absorbed in bel canto arias at a Steinway grand.

The singer was not oblivious to this mockery, but whenever she gazed out from her piano through the open windows at their curved backs, some quivering with repressed laughter between the beds, the mere fact that she had an audience—any audience!— seemed always to mean more to her than admiration or applause.

Among the most eager pickers were two of my father's victims: the seamstress and her deaf daughter. They would carry their strawberries home in baskets woven from strips of waste plastic and never picked more than these baskets could hold. The children of the turbine attendant and his drowned Iraqi wife must surely have heard the teacher's arias too, but I have no memory of them. While picking strawberries myself, I often wondered whether there was something—a vibration, a caress of the eardrum, a vestige of a song—that the seamstress' deaf daughter could *hear* or feel of those shrill arias. Now I dream of water roaring in the drowning, suffocating girl's auditory canals and in her perforated oral cavities, and some nights these dreams startle me from sleep and keep me awake.

Although the gathering of inadvertent witnesses of my father's act that St Nepomuk's Day in May had never suspected anything, perhaps in the continuing belief that it was a complete accident, a concatenation of fatal circumstances or indeed a *tragedy* which cost this wretched, marked man his own life a year after the disaster at the Great Falls, my investigations so far leave little doubt as to his guilt.

From my camp on the Rio Xingu, I sent an endless stream of questions via malfunctioning satellite connections across the Atlantic to Bandon—to Mira, to those who attended the festival at the Great Falls, to the technicians who maintained the sluice systems, and even to a few horn players from the Rafters' Band who had set their instruments down in shock as my father's victims vanished in the whitewater. And my conclusion was always the same: this wasn't a tragedy, it wasn't an accident—it was a crime.

On what was provisionally the last of my construction projects, at the Tonle Sap's confluence with the Mekong in the Cambodian capital, Phnom Penh, I saw how even mighty rivers reverse their courses under the pressure of water during the rainy season and appear to flow back towards their sources, and I have sworn to myself ever since that I will seek clarity not only about my father's motives for his act but also regarding his puzzling transformation from a man possessed by the past into a man abandoned by his kith and kin and all benign spirits, a man eventually prepared to kill.

TWO

In the Spray

I always feared my father more than I loved him. However much I admired him as he ploughed through the whitewater, zigzagging between rocky stacks and channel markers in a zodiac powered through the spray by two revving outboards, as he used a pickaxe to free some driftwood trapped in a sluice gate or untangled some cables, I was scared stiff when he succumbed to one of his unannounced and often gratuitous outbursts of rage. An offhand word he deemed unacceptable or simply an ambiguous gesture could cause him to yell abuse, a torrent of swearwords or the name of the person who was instantly pronounced guilty or an accursed enemy.

If my name was shouted, I would always brace myself for a slap, a crushing blow, although my father never, ever hit me, my sister Mira or my mother. From the moment Mira broke two bones in quick succession—fracturing first her shin, then the top of her right arm—and was diagnosed in Bandon's military hospital with a disease whose strange name—brittle-bone syndrome—no one in our family had ever heard before, neither my father nor any teacher in the county would have dared to defy a uniformed doctor's emphatic warnings and hit her or even grab or shove her in punishment. A point mutation in Mira's genome had apparently rendered her bone structure so fragile that her arms, legs, fingers and ribs could break under the slightest pressure. It was true that on an X-ray image that my sister had pinned to her bedroom wall after a series of examinations her ribcage looked as if it were made of frosted glass; even a playful wrestle could cause bone splinters to puncture her lung or—as she put it—pierce her heart.

Ever since the original diagnosis, Mira had cherished the special or even precious status this disease conferred on her, and I had envied her. Bones of glass suggested a filigree, tinkling aristocracy and made a sufferer not deplorable but unassailable. A mythical creature. A fairy.

In addition, the extent of the defect seemed to decrease after the first bone fractures. This improvement was, in fact, merely the result of extreme caution and an almost hysterical wariness that transformed her vulnerability into virtuosic agility. Over time, she was able to evade even a feinted punch or kick with nimble certainty, *flying* away from threats so fleetly and alertly that even a flash attack would have struck only thin air.

Only once was she not quick enough after that first battery of examinations and results at Bandon hospital. A riverside rock cracked under our weight as we were fishing for rainbow trout together below the Great Falls, and unable to reach the bank fast enough, she jumped off into the supposedly more forgiving dark waters, shattering her collarbone on a reef hidden under gurgling eddies.

Mira was inviolate, and yet an angry outburst from our father could rob her (like anyone else in the firing line) of words and breath, and she would forget that his shouting had never led to violence.

I remember one autumn morning when Mira's tomcat—a present from the coloratura-singing strawberry woman—ran along the wide, frost-furred handrail of the jetty connecting the lockmaster's house to one of the boat channels, clutching a common dipper in its mouth. My father was just shutting the icy gate of the boathouse when he caught sight of the tomcat, known as Tiger due to its markings, with its prey. My father revered birds; he loved them. He didn't need to hear their singing to recognize the songbirds of the riparian forests, only their warning cries, and it had taken all my mother's talents of persuasion to convince him to let Mira accept the gift—an enemy of birds—from the strawberry house.

As the tomcat came towards him along the handrail, triumphantly parading its prize, my father did not roar the hunter's name or any other word but gave a hoarse yell that drowned out even the whitewater thundering below the jetty. Tiger instantly dropped the bloodied dipper, which was still alive but could no longer fly, and attempted to spin around on the handrail and flee from this roaring ball of rage, but in doing so lost his balance and plunged in panicked contortions into the rapids after his tumbling prey and was lost for ever in the seething whiteness.

Mira and I looked for Tiger for many hours and repeatedly in the following days until, having already given up hope of saving the cat, we were forbidden from extending our search to inaccessible and rocky sections of riverbank with the more modest aim of erecting a shrine to our father's victim. A standing stone around which we wove moss and swallow-wort gentian and decorated, until the first snow, with fresh fir twigs and heather was the only permitted memorial to Tiger.

That autumn, I was just learning to read. Until then my sister, four years my senior, had described scenes from river tales or adventures involving underwater beings to me in a variety of protagonists' voices—high-pitched, croaky, or as deep as she could possibly go. Inspired by Mira's thrilling theatre, which she performed in our shared bedroom each night before we went to sleep, I spoke for several days after Tiger's watery end in the voice of an evil sorcerer lurking on the riverbed. I shouted, I cried and I purred until my sister told me that my screeching was not modelled on any fairy-tale figure but on our father.

I never completely relinquished a thought that pursued me even in my dreams back then—the thought that my father did not have to hit, wound or threaten anyone with an axe, a knife or other weapons because he only had to use the overwhelming power of his voice to *bawl* someone who'd prompted his rage into flight— or to death. Even when he sang his embellished, improvised version of a many-versed river song to the accompaniment of the button accordion, which an engineer from Hydroelectric Plant IV played at our table on the occasional Saturday night, I sometimes believed I could still detect the tremors of his outbursts capable of convincing anyone who heard them that at any moment they might be plunged into a void, into a raging torrent, into the abyss.

A few days before she left my father, before she was forced to leave us all and return to her Adriatic homeland in a convoy of five deportation buses, I heard my mother whisper the word *devil*: my father was a devil. And I believed then that I had finally found an explanation for his baffling transformations—from a laughing playmate into a furious demon; from a man who would be silent for days or lenient into a singer who wailed river songs; from a lockmaster who rode through the spray in a dinghy into a fearful landlubber who never approached water without a cork lifejacket: he was *the* devil. His voice could make any sound, he could assume any shape. No one but the devil could in one moment appear as St Nepomuk, and in the next as an executioner who weighed down a trussed-up victim with stones and pushed him into the water. No one but the devil could take the form of a waterlily, and in the next instant become a buzzing dragonfly, a kingfisher, a bloodthirsty troll, a murmuring seducer showering his bewitched prey with white rose petals.

Perhaps, I realized in the sleepless nights of my first months working as a fluid mechanic on the upper reaches of the Blue Nile—perhaps my father's irascibility was also just an expression of his helplessness in the face of the fact that times were changing, that the eras of lockmasters and the belief in river spirits were becoming irrevocably consigned to the past, that he was incapable of holding on to my mother or any other person he loved for ever, and that what appeared to be the present was tumbling and racing past him as irretrievably as the waters of the White River.

What is clear is that my own sometimes seething, occasionally suffocating rage as a child was, in a sense, a continuation of my father's wrath, an affiliation as distinct as the odd line or shadow in my facial features which, year by year, increasingly resembled his. Possibly in despair at my mother's disappearance, possibly as a show of force to offset my fear of my father's outbursts, I began to kill.

Some of my childhood memories often appear to me as if veiled in the same spray that repeatedly enveloped the lockmaster's house or, when the winter sun hung low, cloaked it in a gauze of prismatic colours; in some of my mental images, even my father's sunburnt, bony face is unclear, twisted into a pitying mask as he watched one of my attempts to cut flying hornets in half with a pair of scissors.

He would suck in air through clenched teeth as if in sudden pain and shut his eyes. The almost imperceptible whistle as he seemingly drew breath for his pity was all anyone heard of his sigh. And by the time this man I so often feared opened his eyes again, I had either managed to cut the insect down in mid-flight or, far more frequently, had missed and then snapped the scissors shut to form a dagger with which I stabbed angrily at the air. Not once did my father offer any comment, nor did he try to discourage my attacks. In those moments, I was the devil and he a mere witness to my murderous instincts.

As a child and even as a hydraulics student, I killed a lot. Of the many animals that fell victim to my hunting or their roles in my lethal games, hornets were my most dangerous foes. I had deciphered an unsettling inscription on a monument at Bandon ferry terminal in memory of a bloody skirmish near the headwaters of the White River that seemed to offer divine endorsement of my anger. The monument consisted of a poured-concrete figure of a dying army frogman in a landing craft. His head was resting in the lap of an angel, and an Old Testament quote was carved into the side of the boat. Only years later did I discover the source of those menacing lines:

So shall the Lord, your almighty God, deal with all your enemies. He will send hornets among them so that all shall be killed, even those who flee and those who seek in vain to hide. Do not be afraid. Your great and terrible God is with you.

I remember that I had to ask Mira for help in my first attempt to read this memorial before running my fingers over the moss-covered letters of this quotation carved or chiselled into the concrete, as if caressing a petrified, small furry animal.

Almost every day of summer, I would chase with open scissors the scouts that preceded swarms of hornets buzzing along the south side of the lockmaster's house, looking for an old entrance hole or a safe place to build a new, grey, hanging fortress. Mira never participated in these hunts because she did not want to risk her brittle bones at what she considered a pointless game and was not interested either in adventures that demanded only extreme speed and no nimbleness; she did constantly warn me about threatening counterattacks by my victims, however. Yet I dismissed these warnings as attempts to devalue my superiority in one of the few disciplines in which I outshone my sister.

A few scout hornets and the pursuing swarm became the only prey ever to resist my murderous intent, almost killing me in a frenzied Sunday-morning counterattack. Seven of them stung me so many times on the neck, wrist and temples that my father wrapped me in wet, ice-cold towels and laid me in the back of his pickup because I could only breathe lying down. My fingers were still clasping the handles of the scissor. Not even my mother could loosen them as she cradled me in her arms like the angel on the monument. Helicopters couldn't land in the gorge by the Great Falls, so I had to be driven at great speed up a steep track to the edge of the ravine. I saw the trees along the sides of the track racing past like a massive palisade. My mother bent over me, clasping my scissor hand, showered me with pet names, and when I closed my eyes, talked frantically to me to keep me from falling unconscious and potentially choking to death.

On the large panoramic terrace of The Falls restaurant, a former rafters' tavern offering spectacular views of the water spectacle far below, I was strapped to a stretcher in one of the rescue helicopters at which I had so often aimed and fired imaginary salvos from my outstretched arm from down in the gorge. The helicopter had flown up from a downriver hospice, whose residents were mostly staff from the hydroelectric stations and power engineers dozing through the last days of their lives.

From that Sunday on, each time we drove past the rafters' tavern, frequented now by kayakers and divers, or had a celebration dinner out on the viewing terrace, my mother would remark that here, high above the Great Falls, I had been granted a second life, and every time we came up here was like a birthday. And my father would pronounce the same, unchanging words, as if this were a ceremonial dialogue: *From spray we come, and to spray we shall return.* It was a line from one of the river songs he used to sing along to the button accordion.

The thundering of the Great Falls could be heard up on the mossy concrete terraces near the scene of my rebirth, but in the lock-master's house at the bottom of the gorge it was so deafening that even my mild-mannered mother sometimes had to shout. She shouted if she was trying to mollify me and beg for mercy for my victims. Mercy for houseflies and wild bees, which I caught with a tin cup against the windowpane and drowned in hot water or in a shot of brandy. Mercy for slowworms, frogs and dragonflies, but mainly for fieldmice, which I left trembling in agony in live traps before showing the prisoners to the tomcat to rouse his bloodlust. Soon, I would open the barred door of their jail and shoo the fieldmice to their deaths.

Mesmerized by the cruelty with which Tiger caught the released rodents and then repeatedly allowed them to escape his claws to practise his hunting skills, I remained insensitive to my mother's pleas for mercy. If she tried to pre-empt the spectacle by engineering the release of a trapped victim before it could be delivered up to the tomcat, I would take my trap off to my secret arena—a rocky ledge by the river where I forced the fieldmice to fight wild animals as the *gladiators* or *slaves* of my imagination.

But the tomcat—my tiger in this spectacle, my lion, my beast—also pointed the way out of sheer bloodlust by demonstrating, after atrocious hunting scenes and feigned releases, how to break the prey's neck with a single bite and then devour it. This devouring to stay alive and survive, and nature's indifference to the victims' suffering, served as my ultimate justification for toying with death.

In the water meadows along the White River, upstream from the Great Falls, I began to lie in wait on a grass-covered rock jutting out of the water and catch rainbow trout and brook trout with my bare hands. I would often dangle my hand in the water for half an hour or more until the fish swimming in the current grew accustomed to the motionless claw—and gradually forgot about it. I was able to guide my thumb and forefinger slowly, very slowly, like a pincer, along the gently undulating tail and dorsal fins to the fanning gills, then suddenly, with an excited cry, close my fist and hurl my catch out of its element onto the grass.

The writhing, slimy fish disgusted me, so I chose not to break its spine or smash its head on a stone but let it asphyxiate in the grass, watched its rainbow skin dull and its eyes lose their gleam, then stuck a debarked stick into the gullet of my finally inert catch and grilled it, sometimes until it was charred, on a drift-wood-strewn gravel bank.

My fire always blazed more brightly than the size of my prey required, as if the flames were not supposed to cook the white flesh but destroy the evidence of my crime. I threw stones at emperor dragonflies fleeing the rising smoke in flashing manoeuvres, and sometimes I would weep at my situation when I removed my disfigured victims from the embers and, full of loathing, begin to eat them.

My mother left Bandon county, left my father, left her fragile daughter and me in a deportation convoy of five buses in the pouring rain. It was a cold late-October morning that will surely stick in my mind long after the memories of every other day of my life have faded away. I was convinced back then that my mother boarded the second of those buses not only due to a cruel law but also due to the emptiness and silence; the chasm between her and my father, which Mira and I saw widening day by day, had become unbridgeable, and my sister and I could no longer alleviate her desolation.

My father and Jana had hardly said a word to each other in months, slept in bedrooms at opposite ends of the house and indeed only had their meals when the other left the table. And yet, despite their love souring into animosity and silence, Jana was in fact simply complying with the law by returning to her Adriatic homeland. The quotas regulating the number of refugees—derisively referred to as *barbarians*—from war or disaster zones, or those who had sought refuge here for other reasons, had been cut only two years after the previous reduction. *Had to be cut*, in the phrasing of official announcements, illustrated with statistical bar charts, line graphs and occasionally photos of hopelessly overflowing camps flashing up on our screens three times a day to the opening strains of Bandon's anthem.

In my father's schoolbooks—the last mouldy books in the lockmaster's house where, as in other houses in the county, writings and news were read mainly on screens or projected onto surfaces, seldom on paper by then—these quota regulations were called by an old-fashioned and almost forgotten name: *cleansing*. For the plethora of nationalities, clans, tribes and microstates, including Bandon county, into which Europe and then the North American continent had disintegrated in a slow-motion process lasting decades, each separatist fragment of bygone glory—a day's jeep drive from end to end—took pains to distinguish itself from other fragments and to portray its own splendour, its own history and significance in the most brilliant light possible.

Commissariats, republics, counties, alpine districts, matriarchies, patriarchies, duchies and whatever other names these pygmies gave themselves: every little shard wanted its own anthem, its own grotesquely costumed military—armed to the teeth and indebted up to its neck—its own heraldry and, above all, its own triumphant history, wanted to have carved its very own special, heroically winding evolutionary path from horde of apes to belligerent microstate. However distinct all these microstates arrayed along thousands of miles of riverbank were, all these tribes and clans and malignant dwarf empires celebrated their supposed uniqueness, each of these shards of an almost forgotten continental entity clung with near-fanatical tenacity to the belief that all the others ranked below it in the world order. *Its* status alone was dazzling, and its brilliance had to be defended by all possible means against the inferiority of the rest of the world.

Since the end of the age of fossil fuels, when *water wars* had begun to break out in Asia and Africa and also on a tattered European continent, even the stupidest despot had realized that both life and power came from water and ended not just in estuaries and deltas but also above dams and deviated rivers and tributaries. Only those who possessed freshwater and were capable of selling it via leakproof pipes to drought regions or dust-bedevilled deserts could become or remain rich. Even if seawater could be desalinated and, if absolutely necessary, made potable, when compared with the transparency of the White River, this tasteless, additive-poisoned soup was little better than tin or lead when compared with gold.

Although counts and princes and kings had ceased to exist while my father was at school, replaced by corrupt curators and custodians, many of them elected for life, the old names, wreathed with the laurels of memory, had been revived as part of the new world order. Names such as *duchy* and *county*.

Bandon county, for example.

Oddly, the ridiculousness of this frenzy of pompous naming had only struck me during the years I had spent by the great rivers of Brazil, Africa and Asia. On a continental and even a global scale, large corporations had long ruled the water and energy sectors, disregarding the laws and constitutions of a hundred regional parliaments in the interests of invisible shareholder meetings and, if need be, ignoring awkward directives without this impeding their lucrative schemes. In most cases, they could simply acquire anything that got in their way—acquire and then abolish. After all, absolutely everything had a price.

As the continents were once more enmeshed in an infinite tangle of borders, and a gradual and insidious process of miscegenation threatened to muddy the purity of some *distinctive essence*, of some pygmy state, quotas justified the scouring of endangered areas to restore a purity safeguarded by laws and regulations.

Having found refuge in three successive commissariats and finally in our county after the Fourth Dalmatian War in which she lost her parents, two of her brothers and many friends to bombardments, sniper fire and exploding mines, my mother Jana was bought out of a reception camp by my father on the condition that the agreement would expire when the quota came up for renewal.

My father had been looking for a graphic designer for the Great Falls Museum and was convinced that future quota revisions would not affect such rare qualifications as the graphic-design diploma my mother possessed. And so my mother came to the lockmaster's house under the threat of revocation but in the hope of being able to lead a life without the constant threat of expiring deadlines.

Yet, had it not been for Mira and me, she would probably have quit this life and left her lockmaster, the guarantor of her safety, long before her repatriation on that cold October day. As she boarded the second bus of the waiting convoy after we had travelled up to The Falls restaurant in the back of the pickup, she was obliged to leave behind the very people—her two children, born in the spray—on whose account she had endured the thunder of the Great Falls for so many years.

On that drive up to the edge of the gorge, Jana, Mira and I had huddled together under a tarpaulin, hoping that the journey would never end so that we might nestle with our mother in that half-darkness for ever, as if it were a hiding place beyond the reach of any law. Although the rain had gouged deep ruts in the track and our journey was bumpy and punctuated by incessant jolts, I don't think my father looked around even once at his family through the back window of the driver's cab.

Mira and I would have given anything to make the journey to the sea with Jana, to escape to the sea for good. But anyone who was born on this stretch of the White River was considered *pure* and was not only allowed to stay but was required to. The one job, the one assignment that could take natives to a different part of the continent or even farther afield was work involving water, which, in recent decades of natural and civilizational disasters, had become the most precious resource of all.

As our mother boarded the bus with a bag so small that the uniformed driver slammed the door of the baggage hold that had been open when we arrived, and as the bus' folding doors closed with a long hiss, the dark, almost-black tinted windows made it impossible to tell whether the vehicle was empty or carrying only my mother, only Jana. Mira shaded her face with her hands, as if that impenetrable reflective surface were dazzling her—and I began to throw stones at the black glass. I wanted that damned glass to shatter, regardless of whether the bus was carrying away just my mother or other unfortunate people as well, who were near her, with her, and could stand by her.

Mira spoke no soothing words as she usually did when I was breaking some rule, and so one stone after another ricocheted back from the black glass at me and my sister.

My father hadn't got out of the pickup to say goodbye. Instead, when we had climbed down from the cargo bed and unloaded Jana's small bag, he had gripped the steering wheel and set off back down into the depths with the engine howling, as if, from that moment on, he wanted nothing more to do with his wife— or with his children either.

Then the bus convoy began to move off. Jana was the only passenger. There was no one left to stop me from running panting alongside the buses as they pulled away, hurling stones at them until the convoy picked up speed and the last of my projectiles fell on empty ground.

THREE

Mesopotamia

Congo.

Amazon.

Yangtze Kiang.

White Nile.

Mekong.

Yenisei.

Amur.

Indus.

Orinoco.

Back when I was studying fluid dynamics, hydraulic engineers kept lists of the names of the great watercourses, and these were traded in mission reports like casino chips of different colours and values. The length and power of a river determined its value, but the working conditions along its banks and affluents counted even more. If water wars were being fought there, battles over floodplains and estuaries, or if there was a risk of riots or internecine unrest due to the evacuation of villages and large towns from the beds of future artificial lakes, then the value of an assignment along embattled stretches of river would rise significantly and might prove helpful when applying for a highly paid follow-up mission in the next *prospective site* for energy production.

In the maze of European microstates, a new aristocratic caste of hydraulic engineers perpetuated an idea of lost grandeur, because, even in counties like Bandon, they were part of the privileged social classes who owned passports that were valid across dozens of borders and sometimes even worldwide. A network of transcontinental water syndicates encouraged the emergence of new elites. Anyone who succeeded in tying his or her life to watercourses and rivers in the service of these syndicates would eventually reach not only the sea but also a level of prosperity or even wealth—and frequently a degree of freedom—that was utopian to any other inhabitant of the coastline or the interior. After centuries of wars and fighting over the most varied forms of energy, over raw materials and irreplaceable fossil resources, it was as if a process of evolution had reassigned to water the importance it had always had for the animal and plant kingdoms—as a contested and precious substance that depended on the rhythm of rains and droughts and seasons, on snowfall and thunderclouds. Water was not just the source of all life but, more than ever, the source of all power and any future.

The volume of precipitation had not diminished, even in bloodier centuries, and although the melting of the glaciers and polar ice had in fact increased the amount of continental freshwater, raising sea levels and flooding entire archipelagos and tens of thousands of miles of coastline, the contamination of stone-age and more ancient aquifers with seeping industrial and other manmade toxins had created a dramatic shortage amid such abundance.

Clean drinking water or purified water was scarce, and only the immensely rich had access to unlimited quantities of it. There was no more precious resource than the water that the hydraulic engineers extracted, stored and pumped into parched landscapes. The warning that even the greatest exploiters would realize one day—that no one could eat money—had been replaced by a kitchen adage: that even the greediest speculator would be forced to admit one day that you couldn't bathe in rivers of gold, no more than you could irrigate a field or slake your thirst from their springs.

The Colombian syndicate had suspended construction of the Rio Xingu dam until a military solution was found to foil attacks by the doomed Kayapó and other forest peoples. As a result, I had spent two months in Bandon county, mainly on the inflow and outflow of the Great Falls, before the transfer to the Mekong, which I had requested while in Brazil, was confirmed. My switch from the Amazon to the *Mother of Rivers* had been successful because the number of *source seals* in my mission documents already exceeded a hundred, certifying my eligibility to work on any river in the world.

It had been almost two years since my last visit to Bandon, and on arrival I felt as if I had been transported into a different age. Quaking grass waved from some windows of the lockmaster's house, and from a distance I mistook a cushion of moss perched on the threshold of the tool shed for a sleeping animal; the navigation channels, sluice gates and towpaths by which paying visitors could safely approach the spectacle of the Great Falls seemed oddly deserted, although tourists from arid northern regions still stood, like miniature monstrances or fetishes, on the gangways spanning the rapids among the boat sheds, raising their cameras in supplication against the thundering torrent.

I felt like one of those passengers described in school textbooks and physics manuals who returns after years of travelling in a spaceship at the speed of light to find that nothing remains of the world he left behind. Time ran its customary course at the place from which he departed and people were born, grew up, lived their lives, lost their vim and died; but, according to the laws of physics, time had slowed for the passenger during his journey at lightning speed, a single day of his travels passing like a whole year or decade for his contemporaries who had stayed behind on a desertified planet, of which the sole trace on his return was a memory.

The Great Falls Museum was temporarily managed by a retired purification engineer who had no desire to live in damp accommodation amid the spray and therefore performed his daily duties from an antenna-stippled caravan in Bandon. He turned up morning after morning at the measuring stations by the Great Falls, emptied and filled the machines at the lockmaster's house from which visitors could purchase entry tickets, sweets and bottles of flat mineral water, and returned after sundown to his mobile home. Sometimes he did not drive to work in the galvanized, and therefore rust-proof, electric pickup provided by the river authorities, which my father had illicitly lacquered in camouflage colours, but rode down instead on a horse built like battle steed, for which he had rented a box in stables at a Bandon mounted hunting club.

And Mira! My brittle sister Mira was now just a voice on a satellite phone, berating me for my lack of support after our father's disappearance, and for leaving her to clear the house and arrange his affairs alone.

Was I supposed to travel from the Amazon and jeopardize the qualifications and source seals I had earnt on the Rio Xingu, all for a house clearance?

Yes, of course, she said. The lockmaster's house was our home.

So, did she feel abandoned by her brother?

Not abandoned, she said. Left on my own. You left me on my own.

By the Rio Xingu a fully tattooed Amazonian, a man who barely came up to my chest and had been assigned by the syndicate to be our interpreter, spotted Mira's photograph on my draughtsman's table and asked me: *Your girl? Your wife?* Mira was sitting in her kayak, just righting herself after a roll, and inscribing a glittering arc of droplets against the blue of the sky with one end of her double-bladed paddle, as if she, the frail one, were powering across a glassy river. And I had nodded and said: *My girl.*

Mira. What an adventure it was when silently, without a sound, she allowed me to trace river courses, lakes and coastlines on her naked, sun-warmed tummy with the tip of my tongue on one of our summer afternoons on the banks of the White River. What a smooth and fragrant canvas, warmed by a star only eight light minutes distant.

But during our radio conversation Mira had seemed impossibly far away. I would have loved to have taken her in my arms as I used to whenever something worried, scared or troubled me, and I found refuge with her. When I then lay down on her bed, she would sometimes lean over me and allow one strand of her hair after another to brush my face in a curtain fragrant with water and lavender soap and whisper: *No one can see you. Only me. No one can find you. Only me. No one knows where you are. Only me. I make you invisible. You are invisible.*

However, while I was still cursing the tropical downpours at a camp on the Rio Xingu, she had followed a highly decorated dyke reeve to a commissariat at the mouth of the Elbe and, as his wife, acquired a new citizenship without which she would never have obtained a residence permit; but ever since, she had been refused the necessary travel documents for Bandon. Trench warfare around the source of the White River prevented virtually all civilian travel. Three different armies were fighting over marshy terrain, their size risible by Brazilian standards, their shootouts in the riparian forests more like gang warfare between uniformed thugs and hired killers. To pass through the roadblocks and checkpoints and mined no man's land you needed to be able to present papers like mine— those of an untouchable hydraulic engineer.

This then was the situation on my return from Amazonia: my father, Jana, Mira . . . everyone and everything that had seemed part of a distant yet reachable present during those boiling days by the Rio Xingo suddenly belonged to the past.

I found the fly-fishermen (another former turbine engineer at one of the White River's hydroelectric plants) who had seen my father being sucked towards the Great Falls across the mirror-like river waters and had shouted vain warnings at him. He described how motionless this boatman had been as he *flew* along the middle of the river towards the edge of the abyss.

The man, the angler said as he plucked downy feathers with a pair of tweezers from a plywood box before tying them into an elaborate fly, the man had not corrected the course of the lighter with his oar, even when the current span the vessel and pulled him towards disaster with his back to the waterfall. Frozen—yes, like a statue clutching the steering oar in both hands without moving it; the lockmaster, whom he eventually recognized, despite the great distance, by his blue helmet and of course by the ceremonial barge, had surrendered to the extraordinary force of the White River without the slightest resistance.

Flying to his death with his back to the Great Falls. Maybe, I thought, as the angler's voice grew quieter and quieter and gradually dissipated in the roar of a sudden downpour, maybe even a man committing suicide could not stomach the sight of the white depths which sent clouds of spray smoking up like a titan's breath. After all, people who leapt to their deaths from a tower or from the edge of a gorge often closed their eyes before they abandoned their final foothold.

In the following days, I sat for hours with my father's temporary successor outside his caravan and let him describe the circumstances of the accident. But I had heard what he told me long before from Mira and the other participants in the *water festival* on St Nepomuk's Day. His successor had observed no hint of any error or any blame on my father's part. Nor did he hear any cries for help from the people who had capsized, he said, only the screams of horror by the festival-goers gathered on the banks and a noise reminiscent of distant thunder as the powerful current smashed the drifting, upturned lighter into the first of the rocks on which it would ultimately shatter.

I paid a visit to the strawberry woman's daughter, who instead of strawberries now grew lavender in her beds and buddleia that attracted fluttering peacock butterflies. No piano music or singing came through the open windows; there were no more sweet berries to pick, and no audience either.

I hiked upstream and downstream for days on both banks of the White River without finding the smallest remnant, one scrap of clothing or splinter of wood from the lighter, and on these walks through tangled brambles and curtains of liana, I found not a single clue that might have suggested anything other than an accident.

In some witness statements, such as the one given by a musician who had played the tuba outside the portal of the rafters' chapel, my father was even portrayed as a *hero*, who had tried to the last to control the swirling surge of water that had capsized the lighter laden with festival guests by closing a sluice gate in a bid to stave off disaster. A chain had snapped during his attempt, the tuba player said—I had already been told this by other witnesses of the accident in Bandon—and broken my father's wrist, turning him into a martyr, a tragic figure crushed by this catastrophe at the Great Falls.

I could therefore have added another bouquet or a solar-powered *eternal flame* to the dried-up bunches and plastic flowers that had gathered under the stone tablet bearing my father's name as the latest victim of the Great Falls and prepared for my departure to the Mekong—if, on one of the final days of my stay in Bandon, I hadn't made a discovery that altered all my assumptions and appraisals of what had occurred that St Nepomuk's Day. Suddenly, everything changed.

On that late summer's day, I was paddling in one of the kayaks in which Mira and I had often *danced* through the whitewater, through familiar whirlpools and eddies below the Great Falls. We had referred to these trips as *dancing* because we would circle each other in our separate crafts or follow each other to an agreed point, a rock or a protruding channel marker. This dance was one of my sister's most impressive performances and triumphs over her brittle bones. Although a single blow of her paddle on a rock concealed by the rapids would have broken her arm, in all my years on the river I have never seen anyone steer a boat as delicately, indeed as gracefully as Mira through the crisscrossing currents. She also taught me everything I know about paddling, rolls and other whitewater manoeuvres.

Although my father's successor no longer stored the fleet of kayaks that had once been at the disposal of visitors to the Great Falls for guided explorations of the *slack*—meaning, calm—water in a corrugated-iron shed, there were still six kayaks hanging there. And as I pulled out Mira's violet-coloured single kayak, there was no one around to authorize or prevent me from doing so. None of the boats had a spray deck, though, so I was bound to get wet in the foaming water. But it was a warm day and the water temperature of just under 20 degrees was still almost summery.

On affluents and oxbow lakes along the Rio Xingu, I had often slid through the calm, black water in a canoe with a single-bladed paddle, and sitting in a kayak again now after such a long time, I felt the wildness and force of the White River. Heeding Mira's lessons about the advantages of minimal effort, I corrected only the water's most violent jolts and blows, and tended to eschew paddling in favour of surrendering to the main flow which rapidly swept me not out of earshot but certainly out of sight of the Great Falls towards those elongated gravelly shoals and sandbanks where I used to land with my father on our dinghy outings. We had lit fires and grilled fish caught on the way. Getting back had been easy thanks to the outboards. What a pleasure it had been to *ride* into the tumultuous current. That day, on the other hand, I wanted to use a hydrographic station two hours downstream and return to my starting point at the Great Falls with a local bus that could transport canoes, dinghies and kayaks in a steel basket on the back.

The strip of sky above the deep-sunk riverbed was cloudless, the change to autumn perceptible only by the sudden drop in temperature, when I glided out of patches of glittering, sunlit water into the wooded shade along the banks. The birdsong appeared to have already fallen silent for this year—no songs, no mating calls, only the occasional warning cry or hateful call and a fluttering escape. Then silence again, the only sounds those of the water: a gentle lapping along stretches of grassy bank, the gurgling of a rapid eddy, the distant and gradual rise and fall of the rushing flow with which the river filed away at rocks or detached pebbles from banks of sand and gravel and rolled them along its bed in a crazy game.

After less than an hour's paddling past steep, hazel- and ivy-covered rocky banks, to which every plant had to cling tightly so as not to fall into the deep-back water, *Mesopotamia* hove into view—the Land between Two Rivers. Mesopotamia was the name my father had given this stretched bank of sand, clay and gravel sprawling in the middle of the river like a beached whale. According to this label, looking downriver, to the left it was the Euphrates flowing towards the sea, to the right the Tigris, and between them the Garden of Eden—Paradise. Whenever we approached this island, tipped up the engines, pulled the dinghy onto the land and barbecued rainbow trout and char over a driftwood fire in a circle of soot-stained stones, for once my father's eyes, which seemed, when he was speaking, to reflect so many of the things he hated, looked as if everything was exactly as it ought to be.

Those summer afternoons on the banks of the Land between Two Rivers did indeed seem to be detached from time, undated. The current had gnawed at this island no differently hundreds of years ago than in those particular hours we called the *present*, and while our catch grilled over the embers, I was able to slip into any of the eras or adventures I knew only from my mother's anecdotes or from books. I *was* a river pirate on the Mississippi then, a researcher on the Rio Negro or a Roman explorer who, having searched in vain for a ford, was forced to set up camp in

Mesopotamia and fall to his knees in the sand under the weight of his weaponry.

What my father dreamt, I do not know. But what thrilled us after each of these landings was a game of conception and creation of sorts. In a narrow bay on this island, which could change shape from year to year depending on the level of the torrents of melt-water, there was a mixture of clay, sand and muddy deposits that could, with a little skill, be moulded into almost any imaginable form. My father created winged fish, mallard ducks, cats and dogs, even grey herons standing on legs of willow. I never made it beyond reptiles and amphibians—lizards, snakes, toads and turtles . . . Mammals and birds far exceeded my artistic capabilities. And yet was it not a snake that, in the shade of an apple tree, had succeeded in luring the first human beings out of Paradise? And didn't snakes therefore exert greater power over humans created by a playful God than even a leopard or a wolf?

Jabber away, my father said when I asked him these and other questions during our hours on the gravelly island. Jabber away.

Only later did I realize that my own and my father's animal universes not only emanated from differing degrees of craftsman-ship but, more importantly, also corresponded to different speeds: his creatures flew and jumped and fluttered and darted; mine never moved far from the earth's surface and, at most, became light in water and began to soar when they dived.

Sometimes we hardened our creations by the fire and left them behind in Mesopotamia, which became more and more densely populated over the course of a summer. If a downpour or steady rain didn't liquefy our Garden of Eden, all these creatures would not disappear until the winter or in the meltwaters of the following spring, leaving the Land between Two Rivers as bare and empty as at the beginning of time, in anticipation of a new visit by us, the creators.

That afternoon I pulled my kayak up onto the Mesopotamian beach and collected driftwood for a fire, even though I had caught no fish. The island lay mid-river in the form of a whale that year, and with a little imagination it was even possible to make out something like a fluke at the downstream end. Along its eastern side, meltwater and highwater had washed up a three-foot-high barrier of grey driftwood, battered drinking water canisters and the bleached tatters of a camouflage tarpaulin—more than enough wood for a fire.

I remember the shock that hit me like an electric charge when, in this garbage-streaked mess of branches, roots and beams, I found an arm torn off below the elbow, the fist still clutching the shaft of a shattered steering oar. Before my eyes, half obscured by flotsam, was the arm of a boatman.

I've forgotten how long it took me to recognize this fragment as part of a life-size, baked-clay figure, an artefact whose creator possibly wished the rest of the river world to believe that a man of flesh and blood was holding this oar and steering a boat downstream. Jutting out of the flotsam was also a shattered bow plank, probably part of a lighter. Had a clay man been used for a deliberate deception?

If the intention had been to stage, for the benefit of a fly-fisherman or other witnesses, the spectacle of a suicidal journey by a lockmaster tormented to death by guilt, and then to make the illusory figure vanish for ever, the clay figure was the perfect prop. After plunging over the Great Falls, it would sink into the rapids, and the shards would be dragged along the gravelly, rocky bottom by the current and revert to their previous unmoulded material.

Had my father really thought of all this—and was this fragment washed up on the shore of Mesopotamia just one of those unavoidable pieces of evidence even the most precise and cold-blooded planning could not eliminate? My father had clearly also taken account of the unlikely scenario that the fly-fisherman or some other fortuitous witness might peer through binoculars at the boatman as he glided past in the middle of the river, too far out for any cry to reach him. In any case, the wrist of the truncated clay arm still bore—as an unmistakeable, distinctive mark—the residue of a prominent, red-painted scar, crafted with a sculptor's touch. Was this supposed to be the mark from the lash of the chain that had fractured the heroic lockmaster's wrist as he tried to close a sluice gate on St Nepomuk's Day and, from the perspective of the festival-goers assembled on the banks, save his victims? Save his victims!

The creator of this clay figure, a master of life and death, had given his likeness a blood-red, swollen scar—a characteristic that would be recognized even through binocular lenses. No doubt about it: whatever this sculpture smashed by the current was supposed to fake, it was the spitting image of my father in clay.

FOUR

Reversal of the Current

It was the end of monsoon season during the first of my three working periods in the Kingdom of Cambodia. I was coming from Kampong Thom province, where I had been measuring flow rates for the construction of a chain of gravitation water-vortex power plants, and was planning to spend a few days off in the capital, Phnom Penh, mainly to see the *Water Festival*, the country's largest celebration.

Boatman Nhean, a former teacher on whose houseboat I had spent the previous week, never tired of describing the three-day festival with its dragon-boat races, fireworks, dances, processions and singing as the highpoint of the year and as a great comfort that could even alleviate memories of the reign of terror by the *White Khmer*, a bloody dictatorship I had learnt about in Bandon's schools as little more than a grim rumour of a cruel bygone era.

Jayavarman, a Khmer Blanc general whom his acolytes reverently referred to as *Jaya* and worshipped like a demigod, had adopted the name of the thirteenth-century Khmer king responsible for turning the temple city of Angkor and the Khmer empire into a flourishing power. Jaya ordained that white, the colour of purity, should be the banner under which to fulfil a triumphant return to the past, obscuring the fact that this path had led once before along rivers of blood to a sea of agony at the decree of a farmer's son from Kampong Thom who had also discarded his real name, Saloth Sar, in favour of *Pol Pot*, under which he led an army of butchers, the *Khmer Rouge*, who plunged Cambodia into an unprecedented cataclysm. The true colour of the Khmer Blanc was, however, like that of their red predecessors, the colour of blood.

Over the course of a four-day interrogation by Jaya's henchmen, Nhean had the forefinger, middle finger and ring finger of his right hand amputated with a pair of tin shears, and lying chained to an iron bench in a sludge of faeces, blood, urine and vomit, had whispered, screamed and stammered to his torturers everything they wanted to hear.

Since those days, and on those evenings on the boat when he told me about his life, he could speak only in a stutter. His wife and two daughters had burnt to death along with two other families in a temple the Khmer Blanc had nailed shut from the outside and then set fire to during a raid. And where his house had once stood, there was now just a swamp stained black by charcoal and ashes.

Now this houseboat, its sides painted with the phases of the moon, its palm roof and prayer flags flapping from lengths of string, was his only remaining refuge as it drifted across the great lake between the landing stages of Phnom Penh and Siem Reap, affording him—along with his catch from the fishing he did on his ferry trips—a lonesome life of grief.

On this first evening of the Water Festival, I was sitting, soaked to the skin by a tropical cloudburst, on one of the topmost steps leading down from the palm-lined promenades outside the royal palace to the embankment at the confluence of the Tonle Sap, the *Fresh River*, with the Mekong, and I was suddenly stunned by the certainty that my father was a murderer, a murderer who really had wished for and planned the deaths of five people who drowned in the whitewater of Bandon's Great Falls—planned them like any other undertaking in his life.

It was strange to be transported back to Bandon, to the Great Falls and the rapids that raged around my parents' house from here, under the bouquets of a fireworks show by the Mekong. Overwhelmed by the stream of images that had impressed themselves on my mind during my first months in Cambodia, I had not thought about the sites of my childhood or any of the places that united me with my frail sister Mira and seemed so idyllic from the distant perspective of Cambodia. The black mirrors of the Mekong and the Tonle Sap lay as calm as a lake in the spidery light of the explosions.

Hundreds of thousands of excited people had gathered along the riverbanks, where they appeared as miles-long ribbons of light in the darkness, to celebrate the Bon Om Touk water festival that marked the end of the monsoon and the start of a new season but, above all, the fact that even a great river like the Tonle Sap could reverse its flow—reverse it!—and stream back towards its origins, back to its source and into the past, before coming to its senses at the end of the monsoon, reversing its flow a second time and, at long last, like all water on this earth, heading towards the sea.

For two or three heartbeats, the flaming arches and bridges of light created by the fireworks spanned the banks of the Tonle Sap and the Mekong where the rivers joined in front of the palace, before fading away in a glittering spectacle of colour, and the thunder that rang out after their lightning had beaten the tattoo of the logic-defying act being celebrated here: *the reversal of the current.*

Sitting there in the middle of the cheering crowds, I suddenly thought that I could make out amid the surging applause and the rhythmic chanting the appalled voices of the people who must have witnessed my father's metamorphosis into a murderer on St Nepomuk's Day without fully grasping what was taking place— not an accident, not a disaster, but the drama of one human being rejecting any stirring of pity or empathy to kill another.

I had only learnt of the screaming by the Great Falls from Mira's audio files, which reached me on the Rio Xingu in Brazil as part of her video recordings plagued by faulty reception. But I really did believe that I could hear those horrified cries in the rejoicing of the masses along the riverbanks on the first night of the three-day Water Festival.

Five dead. Perhaps my father had left the number of victims of his opening the side sluices of the cliffside channels to chance— maybe five, maybe three, maybe all twelve passengers of the salt barge that had sped along the channel like a projectile through a gun barrel before capsizing in the maelstrom of the rapids.

Five or seven or twelve cannot have made any difference to him—after all, the precise number of their victims did not bother the bomb planters and well poisoners who were, in those times, bent on drawing attention to themselves and their grand ideas in counties, tribal areas and microstates. Deaths meant fear; and fear meant open ears and open eyes. No one could fail to hear, no one could fail to see what a murderer did, even if he denied his deed.

With this crime, my father clearly wanted to defy the course of time and take himself back to overweening dreams where a lockmaster had been more, much more and more influential than the curator of an open-air museum on the White River could ever be.

A reversal of the current. I had been the only passenger on Nhean's houseboat in the days leading up to the festival. The mutilated teacher had named his craft after his dead wife: *Chantrea.* Moon.

Nhean had not only ferried me back to the capital on the muddy waters of the Tonle Sap from Phnom Penh to Siem Reap, but also, in the process, back through the centuries to the vast expanses of Angkor, the former capital of the Khmer empire, sunk in rainforest crisscrossed by dams and canals. More than anything, though, he had set me on my father's trail.

Back into the past. The monsoon raised the level of Cambodia's lakes and rivers by 30, 40 or 45 feet every year, transforming villages into islands, rice farmers' stilt houses into arks, roads into waterlogged dams, and teak forests into underwater woodlands with banners of algae flying from their canopies and fish laying their eggs among branches that swayed in the wild currents.

Over one-third of Cambodia—I had read this in the files of the syndicate to whom I owed my transfer from Amazonia to a construction site in Kampong Thom province—was submerged in these months by a tide, invoked with rain gongs and prayers, that rose and fell with the precision of a sundial. Without the fertile deposits from these floods, no grass could grow in the pastures for the buffalo and zebu herds, no rice in the bunded paddies; indeed agriculture and, with it, civilization, art and all life's varied pleasures would have remained but dreams in the land of the Khmer.

Most of all, however, the high-water spate of the Mekong under the mountainous clouds of the rainy season became a murky, glassy dam that held back the Tonle Sap at its confluence outside the palace and prevented the gentler, weaker river from entering their shared bed, compelling it to reverse its course, forcing it onto a huge flood basin, a lake, that could expand to seven times its original size during the rains. This lake lay like a periodically throbbing watery heart in the centre of Cambodia, lapping at the boundary walls of what had once been considered the greatest, most magnificent city in the world: Angkor.

In the Khmer language, Boatman Nhean said, Tonle Sap meant *River without Salt*, but fishermen and ferrymen like him called it, with something like fondness, *Fresh River*. During the monsoon, it rushed out of the cloud-veiled rainforests of its head-waters over dams and weirs, grew gentler as it flowed onwards, sank, now babbling with exhaustion towards its mouth before the residence of the Khmer kings, once worshipped as gods, in Phnom Penh and then paused, barely a day's walk from the surf of the

South China Sea. Paused, as though fearful of the ocean's proximity, smoothed itself out, stood still—and began, under pressure from the Mekong, to flow for months slowly and inexorably back towards its origins until, at the end of the rainy season, the power of the Mekong waned and it once more reversed its flow and turned away from its sources and back towards the sea.

And while water levels fell and the floodwaters from the interior drained away so quickly that shoals of fish were trapped in bushes and treetops as in nets, and were plucked from the branches like fruit by the inhabitants of floating villages, the land-scape re-emerged from the floods as if some cyclical tectonic force were liberating boat routes from the weight of water and turning them back into roads and tracks, islands into undulating plains, causing fields and pastures to push up through a cloud mirror, framed by boggy banks, towards the sky.

Reversal of the current. By the human sacrifice with which he had rejected reason and humanity on St Nepomuk's Day—this was the conclusion I arrived at on Nhean's boat—my father had sought to elevate himself above the age in which his birth had trapped him. Back. He wanted to escape his present and go back to the glories of the past, so that he might return to being what the lock-masters of previous centuries had been with their art of controlling the White River: masters of life and death.

Nhean, who after those days of interrogation had been com-pelled to transfer all the lost abilities of his right hand into his left one, accompanied me, finally stammering out the story of his torments and those of his family, to the temple city of Angkor Wat, besieged jointly by the forest, pilgrims and tourists; and during our evenings on the boat and through restless nights plagued by swarms of mosquitoes and insomnia, described the reversal of the current as a blessing granted to his people and to anyone who surrendered to the pull of the heavens and the ocean instead of fighting against them.

On that first night of the Water Festival, Nhean crouched a few steps below me on the bank of the Mekong and carefully set a little ship made of bamboo and banana leaves on the waves. He held his right arm protectively outstretched, its two fingers unscathed by torture reminiscent of a claw, watching motionlessly as the vessel laden with flickering wax candles and lotus flowers floated downstream, was caught by a lazy eddy, then capsized and disappeared bottom-up into the darkness.

Only then did he lower his arm, stood up and bowed to the waters in gratitude. The Mekong had accepted his sacrifice—a scale replica of the houseboat, with its roof of corrugated iron and palm fronds, on which we had spent the previous days.

Nhean had offered his services when I arrived from Kampong Thom at a floodlit bus station in Phnom Penh, the terminus of an exhausting journey, and I had accepted his offer as if among all the waiting hawkers, yelling accommodation arrangers, rickshaw and taxi drivers, the two of us had an appointment. From my step I now saw the fireworks reflected in the trickles of sweat creeping down his forehead and cheeks as an innate sign that this man came from a watery realm, belonged to water and remained bound to water, like the shattering mirror of the Mekong which cast back the firework patterns into the night sky as splinters of light and fragmented flashes.

Nowhere in Cambodia, Nhean had said that afternoon on the way to the landing stages, was the spectacle of the *reversal* more dramatic than in front of the royal palace here in Phnom Penh. For in front of this palace the Mekong shared a mighty bed for half a mile with the Tonle Sap. And when every year the Mekong in spate blocked the Tonle Sap and began to force it back, this reversal commemorated the merciless barbarism of the Khmer Rouge and Khmer Blanc who, blinded by past glories, had committed genocide, robbed him of his wife, his children, his house and a good life, and mutilated him.

Hadn't these barbarians wanted at all costs to return to the old Angkor, which in the twelfth century had been home to over a million people and was once the most magnificent imperial city in the world? And in their desire to achieve that long-gone imperial splendour, they had followed the example of the Tonle Sap, but only in one direction, forgetting that the river turned a second time in the course of one year, and only thus could the balanced order of life be restored.

When the Tonle Sap obeyed the royal order shouted from the palace on *Bon Om Touk* and *converted* and merged with the Mekong rather than retreating from it, Nhean said, it was allowed, as if transformed by this fresh reversal, to leave their shared riverbed after half a mile and wind its own way, under a new name, towards the mangrove forests of the Cambodian coast.

53

Châktomuk, Four Faces, is what the Khmer called the pitted cross formed by the confluence of two rivers, a cross that had not only etched itself into the muddy ground of the empires of Angkor's god-kings but also into the blood-soaked reigns of terror of Pol Pot and his no-less-past-obsessed successor, Jaya.

It is a murky cross, deeply carved by whirlpools and eddies, into which the Tonle Sap—the only river in the world that reverses its course twice in tune with the seasons—vanishes almost without a sound. A river which appears to return to its headwaters but then, as though coming to its senses, strives towards the sea kept reminding me, in those sleepless nights on Nhean's boat, of other about-turns that seemed to contradict the laws of physics and logic—for example, a thundery shower sucked back into the clouds, paths back to the origins of organic life or into the deep sea, paths back into childhood . . . or into a lost paradise.

Jaya, Nhean had stuttered, had seen the current reversal as the only pointer back into the past, and as Cambodia's future. And just as the old Khmer empires had arisen from paddy fields, palm groves, gardens and pastures for livestock, Jaya's doctrine suggested that a new dictatorship governing the whole of Indochina should flower from farm work too.

People living in the cities, among them 13 of the boatman's relatives, had been driven out into the countryside and forests and to the coast in their hundreds of thousands by Jaya's soldiers. They were to become farmers, workers, fishermen, and the jungle was to become arable land, the wilderness a garden. But who from the city knew how to plant rice, fell trees, cultivate and irrigate fields?

Glasses, Nhean had said. Anyone wearing glasses was suspected of not being a new revolutionary man but a misguided city-dweller or a recalcitrant brainworker and was crushed. Anyone caught understanding a foreign language, like Nhean, who told me his and his country's story in faltering, American-accented English which he had taught himself on his houseboat from lessons on the Great Net, was suspect and was crushed. For many years Phnom Penh was a ghost town, its deserted streets, overgrown houses, overgrown squares and parks reclaimed by the wilderness, rats, packs of feral dogs and tribes of monkeys. Trees stretched their branches out of broken windows and shattered doors, and mould, orchids and moss advanced over empty bookshelves and tattered wallpaper.

On our boat journey, Nhean had repeated three or four times the names of all thirteen members of his family tortured to death, executed or disappeared, like a litany designed to ward off death; told me about his father bleeding from gunshot wounds in his clay-pit hiding place where he was discovered and buried alive by the Khmer Rouge; told me about his brothers being bludgeoned to death with bamboo rods, and his bruised and battered mother starving amid fertile paddy fields on the shores of the most abundant fishing grounds on Earth because *Angkar*, Jaya's all-powerful party, claimed to take care of everything, everything, and accused the famished people, who picked fruit or gathered snails and worms, of scorning Angkar's boundless care—a crime that could land the accused in the torture cells of Tuol Sleng in Phnom Penh and from there to *Choeung Ek*, a marshy spot near the capital. In Choeung

Ek, *enemies of the people* had to kneel on the edge of a pool and bow their heads as a sign of humility before their skulls were staved in with bamboo clubs, as the Khmer Rouge didn't want to waste cartridges they had dedicated to the revolution on scum.

In the first days after my arrival from Europe, I had seen the blood-spattered walls of the cells and interrogation chambers in Tuol Sleng and the rags of the slain that floated to the surface of the black pool in Choeung Ek like oxygen bubbles and then sank back, floated up and sank back. Strips of fabric, threads, fibres.

During those days with Nhean on the Tonle Sap, whose shifting currents rocked and cradled life in and on the water and yet could not ease the pains of memory, I had washed my clothes, bathed in the eddies and caught snakehead fish in one of the river's countless distributaries and a catfish whose colour was so close to the stilt temples' sacred *white*, the colour of the gods and of purity, that Nhean advised me to throw my catch back into the loamy yellow waters. The only time I ever saw Nhean smile during those days was when talk turned to the upcoming Water Festival.

Beneath the festival's fiery ornaments, he would set a replica of his boat laden with lotuses and lights on the rippling Tonle Sap. And his ship would bob away with many thousands of other flame-bearing rafts and vessels made of banana leaves, bamboo and silk, and this parade of lights would inscribe the reversal of the Khmer river's current into the darkness: a flickering, flowing, fiery symbol to show the hundreds of thousands who had gathered on embankments or moored barges and dugouts to watch this miraculous reversal that nothing—neither water nor time nor life, roaming from sun to sun across the chasms of the sky—advanced in one permanently preordained direction.

His family's murderers, Nhean had said, had wanted to go back from a pathetic, misery-threatened present to the lost grandeur of the Khmer people and the splendours of a forgotten empire. But wasn't death the unchanging sacrifice claimed by every return to the past? Those who longed to return were attracted by a time before their birth and, sooner or later, would be caught by the same undertow as those who pushed forward, come what may, towards a glorious future. This undertow sucked them all into the abyss.

During our days on the water, not a single evening passed without Nhean raving about our destination—the Great Festival— over sticky rice and tea under a petrol lamp hanging from the palm-frond roof; raving with the same sense of anticipation as Mira and I had felt as children in the lead up to *Holy Night*. On Christmas Eve, frost permitting, our mother would pour water over a wire-and-metal Christmas tree erected on the banks of the White River until a sculpture bedecked with icicles and pinecones and glass teardrops, illuminated by hurricane lamps, reminded us of the magic of that night. An almighty being, a god—this was roughly how Nhean understood my memory—had been trans- formed long ago by the light of a shooting star into an infant, lying on a bed of straw, who was worshipped first by mere shep- herds but later by kings.

The Water Festival, on the other hand, was more than anything else a triumph of reason. By ordering the river, from the colonnades of his palace, in a reedy chant to come to its senses and reverse its return to its headwaters, a god-like king had for centuries set an example to those who, like the Tonle Sap, had lost their way: a gentle reversal, a conversion in fact, the path to the sea.

On my missions to the great rivers of South America, Asia and Africa, I have rarely contemplated anything other than technical matters: questions regarding incline, speed of current, the cubic volume of inflow and outflow, gravitation vortexes, varying seasonal depths, pressure ratios and the rotation velocity of turbine wheels . . . In Cambodia, though, in the centre of a maze of feeder channels covering hundreds of square miles that was supposed to supply a series of small gravitation power plants with water from de-mined paddy fields, I had for the first time begun to ask myself a question that disturbed my sleep and my working days and put every technical consideration in the shade.

How thin, perhaps only gossamer-thin, was the membrane separating the essence of a peaceful person who loved music, painting and his children—or at least his livestock—from the beast lurking deep within? And what would it take for this membrane to rupture, to rouse this beast and unleash a maelstrom of contradictory possibilities for a human lifespan?

Weren't the annals of barbarism replete with stories of merciless butchers and mass murderers humming along dreamily to the murmur of romantic overtures, waxing lyrical about their love of

Old Masters' world landscapes rolling off into the blue distance, invoking the magic of birdsong or the floral finery of ancient Chinese-silk carpets? Hadn't some of these monsters proudly shown their terrified visitors photograph albums containing pictures of the most delicate crystalline structures of snowflakes and frost stars which, depending on the conditions of their creation, occurred only once and never again in the entire universe before melting in the warmth of a human breath? And how often had it been recorded that some of the most evil bloodhounds in their dress uniforms jangling with medals and decorations became teary eyed at the sight of a girl stammering a poem of greeting and clutching flowers in her child-sized fist, or bent down to a delighted mother and her infant to pat the baby's wrinkly face contorted by wails?

I had been revising for my final exams at the Hydrological Research Institute in Rotterdam when the International Court of Justice in Singapore, under its Chinese president, finally sentenced the *North American Alliance*, a powerless coalition of four former US states, after more than two centuries of specious justifications and delays, to rehabilitate the mined landscapes and bombed wastelands that the vanished American state had left behind in an almost forgotten war named after *Vietnam*.

Had the legal successors of the former United States not finally been compelled to deal with their legacy, many paddy fields in Laos, Cambodia and Vietnam would have remained lethal terrain for many centuries more and not part of a *promising area* in which hydro-syndicates could build small power plants based on the technical principle of gravitation vortexes. (These power plants could be installed even in virtually flat countryside, and their concrete cylinders—with a diameter of only a dozen feet or so—resembled the plugholes of large sinks in which vortexes, revolving according to the principle of gravity, span the paddle wheels of mini turbines.)

By the time I was awarded my hydraulic-engineering degree, the Singapore judgement had been at least partially enacted. Dozens of hydroelectric missions were indebted to this verdict. The court's experts had calculated that the de-mining would have taken over 300 more years in the circumstances that prevailed *before* this trial, and its verdict—America had to pay no more money for a whole year of de-mining its former enemy state than a single *day of bombing* had eaten up during the Vietnam War.

But now, from the muddy ground of newly accessible paddy fields, around which I steered my dirt-encrusted jeep to the individual construction sites, concrete towers rose into the sky—memorials whose glass sides displayed the skulls and bones of bludgeoned, shot and drowned victims of the Khmer Blanc regime.

My conversations with Nhean and his halting stories had gradually opened my eyes to the fact that my father's derangement was similar to that of the Khmer Rouge and the Khmer Blanc. The membrane between a benevolent life and bestiality ruptured the moment someone obsessed with the past or some other defunct splendour turned away from the present and embraced a reversal of time and a lustre dulled by the centuries. Back! Back and against the current led the path for which the Khmer and my father were willing not just to kill but also to exterminate any creature of the present that was not swept up and carried along like flotsam.

What though, I had begun to wonder in Cambodia, what did the leaders of European nation-states long for; what did the micro-unions and counties proclaimed as a protest against parliamentary democracies, with their mediaeval names and idiotic anthems—what did they desire . . . what were the dreams of the peoples of a continent that had once been smitten with the utopia of unity and was now splintered into hordes and tribes? Wasn't the snap of these flags and pennants, raised on a thousand poles, emblazoned with sewn-on eagles and swords and lions, just the sign of a sinister past?

My father had presumably succumbed to the same current as Pol Pot and Jaya, who had shed their real names as obstacles on their paths into the past. Pol Pot and Jaya had ordered their slaughterers to follow the aberration but not the conversion of the Tonle Sap. Both of them had ultimately fled from Vietnamese and Chinese drone squadrons into the rainforests on the borders of Thailand. Decades later, Pol Pot was discovered there, an old man spouting crazed lectures, but he died in unelucidated circumstances before he could stand trial, and was burnt with his dogmatic writings and some rotting garbage.

The fact that the minions and supporters of these two men had returned from their forest hideouts disguised as farmers, officials and politicians, and lived in the country unpunished, Nhean had added, was a sign that once beasts had crawled out of the innards of their human hosts they never truly went away again, but bided their time in a succession of different costumes.

Him over there, yes, him, that textile trader on the bank, Nhean had said, pointing at a bowed man in a store draped with brightly coloured fluttering scarves, as we floated past after leaving the landing stage in Siem Reap; that man over there, he was one of Nhean's torturers and had wreaked havoc in Tuol Sleng before fleeing from Chinese commandos. Now he traded buffalo-horn carvings and raw silk.

And no one wants to kill him? I had asked. No one wants to take revenge, hand him over to the courts, put him in jail?

If you have suffered barbarism for half your life and are still plagued by nightmares, night after night, Nhean said, you don't want to squander the days of the second half of your life remembering.

And my father? A murderer, I thought; a murderer, I whispered on the palace steps in the night the current reversed, even yelled it once at the thunderous explosion of a spiral of fire whose glittering streams of embers rained down out of a black sky onto the Mekong and scattered before they could touch the river that cast back their light. A murderer. My father was guilty of the death of that turbine warden who had waved his arms in the air twice before his heavy soaked traditional rafter's outfit dragged him under; he was guilty of the deaths of the seamstress and the music teacher who opened her strawberry beds to an audience for piano études—big-hearted women, washed away in their gold-embroidered Sunday best. He was guilty of the death of a trombone player from the Bandon brass band, guilty of the death of the farm mechanic who had frequently repaired my motorbike when I was a hydraulic-engineering student and never charged me. My father was guilty.

That November evening by the Mekong, I was as sure of the malevolence of this vanished man as if a Last Judgement like the one depicted on the altarpiece of the rafters' chapel at the Great Falls had unveiled itself between the monsoon clouds illuminated by fiery corals, shooting stars and sparkling chrysanthemums, and delivered its unanimous verdict. But did I have to yield to this realization like Nhean, who had recognized one of his tormentors and was able to glide past him in his boat without cursing him, without demanding justice and atonement?

I think it was at that moment, on that first evening of the Water Festival, that it dawned on me—as Nhean, a mutilated boatman, set his sacrificial boat laden with wax lamps and lotus on the black waves of the Mekong—that every society produced people who needed killing.

FIVE

Pharaoh and Pharaoh Queen

I had neither heard nor read anything from Mira and her new life at the side of a dyke reeve on the Elbe estuary. Wherever I had attempted to get through to her, screens of various sizes that were supposed to show her face—my notebook plagued by reception failures or the displays of the Cambodian water authorities' new quantum computers—had remained empty and silent.

Even the syndicate's technicians had been unable to find out whether this emptiness and silence was due to recent flare-ups and fighting over access to the North Sea or to a series of explosions in the supposedly de-mined paddy fields of Kampong Thom that had destroyed newly laid glass-fibre cable harnesses. The causes of any interruption in transport or news links were kept scrupulously secret in the Kingdom of Cambodia, as in Bandon or any other musty corner of Europe. Hydraulic engineers like me did enjoy certain economic privileges, but an unlimited entitlement to regional or transregional information streams wasn't one of them.

After trying in vain for two more days to get access from Nhean's houseboat to a news channel so that I could at least have an illegal video conversation with Mira via a meteorological network whose use was restricted to the fishing industry, I had travelled back to my construction site in Kampong Thom in a syndicate van packed with spare parts and measuring instruments. But here too, in a tent pitched on a wooden platform to counter the increased threat of snakes resulting from sinking water levels, I could not accept that it might be Mira herself—and not technological or political issues—who was causing my memories of our life together to gradually twist into crazy dreams and yearnings. I dreamt of her virtually every night, holding her carefully in my arms like a wafer-thin glass sculpture.

Sometimes, during the day, I would imagine her in the wet, figure-hugging clothes of the women who held up plumb lines for channels through paddy fields, along tracks and during brief cloudbursts for me, or angled the mirrors I needed to take my laser measurements. I often undertook these tasks alone because my water-blue shirt with its pattern of white waves was in itself a signal, indeed a request, for every inhabitant to help me or at least to offer me help. I would often simply observe from a mobile platform and bellow my commands over the rice fields and reservoirs through a miniature megaphone.

Mira. When the hours crawled by in those nights under canvas until sleep was finally able to release me or a dream at least numb me, I experienced something like disappointed rage that, despite my many and repeated attempts, my glass sister remained unreachable, invisible, silent. Was it actually for love that she had followed this dyke reeve with his medals, commissions and special permits to the lower stretches of the Elbe—a Friesian who had cut his light-blue-dyed hair in the Iroquois style of the dyke rulers and, like all the syndicate's favourites, knew precious little about the tides, other than that they could rise and fall?

When Mira's message reached me in Brazil, saying that she wanted to leave the lockmaster's house and follow a weir builder, an aristocrat, to the conflict-torn areas around the Elbe estuary, I had consoled myself with the thought that she perhaps only wished to accept some of the benefits, for example: the more convenient regional citizenship, freedom of movement and a more extensive access to communication and entertainment systems. I was convinced, however, that she would return to my side at the earliest opportunity. We were still devoted and indivisibly bound to each other.

Yet, for all her overwhelmingly tender and loving nature, Mira had always been realistic and sometimes shrewd in seeking her own advantage where she could find it. After all, in a divided world like ours, who had ever done or omitted to do something with no expectation of a reward? I had indeed admired Mira's talent for quid pro quo and backscratching until now, in the oppressive nights at Kampong Thom, I was ambushed by the suspicion that I too had become an impediment rather than an aid to her life and might therefore be neglected or even forgotten.

Had the syndicate not warned me twice after my initial refusal to perpetuate the family tradition and take over the office of the missing lockmaster on the White River, approving my application for a transfer from the Amazon to the Mekong only because hiring specialists for local vortex power plants on flat land was like finding the proverbial needle in a haystack?

But how useful was an in-demand specialist with no decorations on his chest, only two severe warnings, to a woman whose main objective was to break free? Moving to the Elbe out of love for a Friesian dyke reeve! No chance—I long regarded this suspicion as a recurring episode from a grotesque dream which disintegrated the moment insects or the cry of a marabou stork woke me in the middle of the night, soaked with sweat.

After the syndicate's decision to entrust me with a construction site on the affluents of the Mekong, Mira and I had agreed to withdraw a route credit from her long untouched air-miles account so that she could visit me one day, possibly a third of the way through my mission in Indochina. Our plan was to kayak through the area known as the *Four Thousand Islands* in the borderlands between Laos and Cambodia, a labyrinthine paradise of waterways. The nights we would spend in hammocks under mosquito nets or in a tent on the edge of water forests; by day we would fish from sandbanks and gravel shoals and cook our catch over an open fire as we had once done on the White River.

This river trip was one of the idle dreams I had harboured among the maze-like Amazonian tributaries in the Kayapó territories but had never realized. However, I had never waited by the Amazon with growing disappointment for Mira to come, because visits by friends and family could disturb the work schedules and were strictly forbidden for someone of my rank. But to the Mekong I had travelled as a hydraulic engineer who, though besmirched by those warnings, had nevertheless been promoted to *streamer* and was therefore entitled to two such visits per year. Ultimately, a needle in a haystack was more valuable than a tailor's pincushion.

The Mekong—as children, Mira and I had read this in a well-thumbed volume of the *Encyclopaedia of Water*, a work whose many volumes were part of the furniture in the lockmaster's house—was nine miles wide in the area along the Laotian border. Dotted around this expanse of water wider than any Mira and I had ever set eyes on, were thousands of islands, most of them uninhabited, which sometimes protruded from the waters like mementos of solid ground during the rainy and dry seasons, only to be submerged again by a surge of high water. The water level of the Mekong rose and fell on a diluvian scale to the alternating rhythm of the monsoon and the dry season, and the resulting increase and decrease in the number of islands blurred any certainty as to what belonged permanently to *terra firma* and what belonged to the river.

The Mekong, a river unspeakably far away in Asia that could expand until it was indistinguishable from a sea and did not threaten to snap closed above our heads like the edges of the White River gorge, became the mythical destination of our dreams. After all, our childhood sky had been a strip framed by two jagged escarpments that only rarely widened to its full extent—and what else we saw of our immediate surroundings was nothing but strips, fragments and segments too.

Mira and I had spent our school years staring at screens in the lockmaster's house and only got a sighting of real-life teachers, along with most other people from the upper world, when we sat for our end-of-term exams at the ministry in Bandon or took part in commemorations of local historical events there. Our father kept not just our mother Jana more or less captive in the ravine by the Great Falls—and anyway, as a foreigner to the county and a southerner to boot! she was not a popular sight in Bandon—but us two children as well, and very rarely were we allowed up into the present day beyond the edges of the gorge.

What we did get to see of the upper world was mainly via our screens or in the form of tourists who marvelled at the sluice gates by the Great Falls from wooden viewing platforms and slender suspension bridges through spray-clouded binoculars and digital cameras. Even the festival-goers who climbed down into our archaic world on St Nepomuk's Day in their rafters' outfits or the silver-embroidered black jackets of salt-quarry squires to applaud ritual lighter rides were not ambassadors of the present but members of the cast of the past.

The tunnels from which the squires had extracted rock salt for boatmen to transport or pumped through brine pipelines had been walled up for centuries by then or were used only as *viewing galleries* in which costumed robots demonstrated the horrors and hardships of salt quarrying. These performances and the *memorial operas* staged on the shores of underground brine lakes were all part of the same glorified remembrance. For whereas other counties, dwarf republics and tribal areas could point to artists, composers, poets, architects or invincible warriors and heroes of science in their midst and call upon them as examples of how sublime a particular continental mini-people was and how superior to another possibly smaller tribe, the only evidence of its own grandeur that Bandon could proffer were salt and the river traffic around the Great Falls. Which is why the county erected memorials and indeed altars to salt—the *White Gold* which had once twinkled on tables and in kitchens, not just across the continent but also around the world, and brought long-eclipsed wealth to Bandon.

As a legal protection of the value of salt, the use of any kind of livestock salt was forbidden on the pastures of meat factories and in the hunting grounds of Bandon; road salt was banned even on icy days; and the cattle in the automated stalls of intensive farms licked a pale-red substitute. Even the pure whiteness of the salt crystals was protected. This salt, we learnt from our school screens, elevated Bandon high above other saltless civilizations and made their culture as insipid and boring as soup that not been enhanced by this White Gold.

But Mira and I hated salt. To us it seemed hardly worth commemorating that this substance had once been extracted or leached from the centre of the mountains and transported on lighters lowered around the Great Falls to the sea and to the tables of emperors and kings. Hadn't far larger barges carried sand, stone and bricks for palaces, fortresses, pyramids and bulwarks down convoluted waterways to gigantic building sites?

While we sat in front of our screens in the lockmaster's house, and Mira aped the solemn tones of a remote teacher praising the *Empire of White Gold* as if it were a paragon of global dominance, the faces she pulled made me laugh so hard that I had trouble breathing. If our mother was nearby, she would warn me of my father's wrath but never utter any reprimand or injunction herself. If our father did catch me scoffing at the glories of Bandon, he would sometimes rebuke me loudly or threaten me with a beating, but, more often than not, he would praise these salt traditions no less solemnly and insistently than our screen teacher. Once our father was out of earshot and sight again, Mira enticed me into fresh giggles by mimicking his sermon, gesticulating and grimacing.

Mira fooled around with me as if I were a soft toy or a wooden mannequin, cajoled me into play fights during which she would knock me to the ground with the lightest of touches; she could make me laugh or cry by reading or reciting a river tale with a sad ending. I obeyed her orders, did whatever she suggested and did nothing she instructed me not to.

Throughout our years at the lockmaster's house, we usually had to keep each other company in our roleplays and escape fantasies, because our need for human interaction was not satisfied by the precious few opportunities we had to speak to other residents of Bandon.

What a ball we had when we were allowed to leave our gorge for the whole afternoon during strawberry season and were free at last to talk and laugh with other people as we bent over the beds of strawberries to the sound of the catwoman's piano-playing and coloratura. This annual convention also attracted our peers—not just *screen pupils* like Mira and I but those taught by real people. We would have loved to invite some of these exotic individuals back to the lockmaster's house, but my father tolerated no visitors from present-day Bandon, arguing that the Great Falls were the only place in Central Europe that had remained untouched over the centuries. It was bad enough that the commissariat allowed fly-fishers, tourists and other intruders to disturb this intact world.

So it soon felt natural to me that Mira and I should turn to each other with growing affection and curiosity, and then with desire and passion. Not only was my sister the most impressive person I knew, she was also—with the exception of the few female strawberry pickers to whom I never dared to speak a word—the only girl I could laugh with, talk to, touch—and embrace.

It was Mira who told me the story of the youthful pharaoh from ancient Egypt in whose memory a monument, flanked by two mulberry trees, had been erected in Bandon, for reasons I came to understand only much later. He was the son of sibling monarchs on the banks of the Nile; he was handsome, powerful and invincible like his parents and, like his father before him, he made his own sister his pharaoh queen and wife. But he died at the youthful age of 19 and was consigned to eternal rest in a king's grave piled high with gold.

Every time Mira showed me the young pharaoh's glittering golden mask on her screen, along with the dried-out, black, mummified skull underneath, I was moved to tears.

Mira's tales of Tutankhamun, that preciously masked dead youth, were in remarkable harmony with the sermons of our screen teachers who spoke of sibling love as an aristocratic, indeed a majestic tradition.

I was already busy preparing to study hydraulic engineering in Rotterdam when I realized that if each of the microstates on the European continent insisted on its own uniqueness and superiority, and tolerated neither foreigners nor immigrants nor refugees nor any other menace to its pre-eminence and magnificence, then logically it had no choice but to rely on its own genes to prolong its survival. Age-old incest bans had stood in the way of this form of population growth, and so most microstates had abolished them long before Mira's birth and mine as no longer consistent with Western traditions.

Our screen teachers did not conceal the fact that these circumstances could lead to an increasing likelihood over the generations of malformations and a wide variety of flaws, but they did make persuasive arguments that this form of demographic growth would distil and quicken what was specifically precious, superior, indeed brilliant and triumphant about us.

Hadn't the pharaohs ruled for millennia in unparalleled splendour over all the lands along the Nile that cyclical floods had made as fertile as the Garden of Eden? What were the ruins of the ancient Greeks and Romans, for example, compared to the palaces and pyramids of the pharaohs, which, though far older, had lost almost none of their majesty and awesome grandeur despite thousands of years of nibbling, biting erosion and destructive wrath?

Our screen teachers' proclamations were also reflected in Bandon's constitution. When Mira and I set out for the catwoman's strawberry fields, the first thing looming before us as we emerged from our gorge was a granite statue of Tutankhamun, engraved in golden lettering and framed by two mulberry trees. And as we continued on our way over a carpet of fallen black berries, resisting the temptation to scoop these watery, sugary fruits into our mouths—after all, a richer, more enticing harvest awaited us among the catwoman's bed, as well as the rare company of strawberry pickers—we left a trail of purple footprints on the cobblestones of Bandon, as if returning to the town from a battlefield.

I only learnt that this pharaoh, revered like a patron saint by the people of Bandon and two other tribal societies, had not only died young but also suffered from deformations including club feet, an oversized pelvis and an ape-like chin, and was only able to walk with the aid of two gilded crutches (which were placed beside him in his coffin) when I got my first ever access to a free internet in the Amazon and decided to show one of the heroes to whom statues of black rock had been erected in my homeland to an officer of the Brazilian security service (who wasn't quite certain where Europe was on the globe).

It is still with an odd combination of shame and excitement that I recall the stormy afternoon I spent with Mira by the White River when the thing I had only dared to imagine before in days and nights plagued by secret guilt actually happened. We had drifted downstream in our kayaks and gone ashore on an elongated sandbank—a beach only we knew and used—to barbecue on one of our old stone-circled fireplaces two rainbow trout we had caught on the way. While I was gathering silvery driftwood, Mira jumped into the crystal-clear, green water of a sidearm of the river that disappeared into the blossoming, thorny branches of the riparian forest.

As I was blowing on the incipient fire, over the first flames I saw Mira swimming towards me from the mouth of the tributary, waving to me and then suddenly diving; she was underwater, invisible, for so long that I had already waded into the water up to my waist, making for the spot where I had last seen her, when she shot out of the reflected clouds only a yard or so from me, her arms outstretched in triumph, with a cry similar to when she used to leap out from behind a door or a curtain. She was naked.

My sister had slipped out of her shell-patterned swimming costume, down in the realm of the crayfish, rainbow trout and bass, and burst panting towards me through skeins of sparkling strands of water. And in those seconds, as my heartbeat raced, I felt that at last I could glimpse the bridge for which I had longed with so much shame in chaotic nights and now only had to stride across it to go from being her brother to being her lover and her pharaoh.

Mira put her arm around me and led me, like a lifeguard leading someone she had just saved from drowning, out of the water onto the shore and there, on a bed of sand and moss, she began to play with me. She played with me as she had when we were small, running her fingers over my hair, my chest, my stomach, tracing circles and spirals around my navel with the tip of her forefinger, and then pretended she had to do mouth-to-mouth resuscitation on the one she had rescued, painting my lips with her tongue and, after her hand had taken a slow and winding path along my whole body, leaving me rigid, almost paralysed with arousal, with no idea how to act in her embrace, she let me sink breathlessly between her open thighs, speckled with droplets of river water, and revert to the state of a moaning, panting infant between her breasts. I moaned, I cried out—I cried out because only a cry could prevent the pressure of unknown lust from blowing me apart.

The sole thought I can remember was the question that swirled among all the river images as to whether the seed I had spent deep inside my sister's rhythmically rocking body might grow into an all-powerful royal child, worshipped as divine, a child of glass who would immortalize its parents, entwined in sibling ecstasy, as gods.

The blissful exhaustion which made me doze off for a few minutes in my pharaoh queen's arms seemed, when I woke up again, to be simply a reminder that in an instant like this everything a human being could desire in life might come true—everything Bandon and the rest of a European continent tormented by fears of death and decline could expect of their children, namely, the survival, the future of a society or a tribe from its own resources— and that the only fitting end to such delights was sleep or maybe merciful, instant death. What else but paradise could follow this afternoon by the White River?

All that followed this ecstasy and bliss, in fact, were memories. There were moments of intimacy with Mira after those hours by the riverside, but never again did she take me in her arms as then, and none of those moments was comparable with what happened in the sand and the moss that afternoon when the water music drowned out the sounds of our passion.

Had Mira merely given her brother a gift of a kind that could be offered only once in life and never again? Those unrepeatable moments froze into crystalline images whose cracks and reflections gradually began to make me wonder whether what had happened had been real—or if it had all been euphoric wishful thinking, just a phantasmagoria. Yet whether it was a memory or true happiness, they both seemed so fragile and precious to me that I never dared to ask Mira—while we were together or in our later digital correspondence—about the difference between reality and dream.

And Mira . . . Mira laughed, Mira pulled my hair, which was shoulder-length in accordance with the latest laws governing anyone born in Bandon, kissed me on the cheek and looked me in the eye, all without even a casual signal whether I and my lust were caught in a fantasy or in the real world.

My only indisputable recollection—indisputable to this day— is the symphonic sound of the White River pouring towards its own dissolution in the sea, enveloping my pharaoh queen and me in its endless arpeggios on an August afternoon flickering with dragonflies, encasing us in a melodious cocoon as it divided thunderously at rocky obstacles or seethed around the stone blocks of towpaths and weirs, every eddy making a different fibre of my being reverberate.

SIX

Four Thousand Islands

Three days after the festival to mark the reversal of the current, I was still waiting, and I waited for a further day and a further nine hours, waited on the riverbank, on the terrace of a tearoom, waited for Mira to ring me from Phnom Penh airport where I was planning to meet her with Nhean to set out for the *Four Thousand Islands*, for reality. But I waited in vain.

Had my sister followed a blue-haired syndicate protégé to the Elbe estuary because she perhaps never had any serious intention of travelling with me through the labyrinth of the Four Thousand Islands? Depending on the level of the Mekong, these islands lay—categorically, and just as we had planned—in varying numbers in the same places and at the same coordinates as cartographers had situated them—our islands! And kayaks lay rocking against jetties built on bamboo stilts in dozens of riverside villages, ready for us and any other visitor to the Mekong, but as I waited, *Si Phan Don*, the name of our island empire, gradually receded into the title of one of those river tales Mira had once read to me, none of which offered a path into real life.

After all the waiting, my eventual decision to depart without Mira gave me 11 days of leave the syndicate had ordered me to take. In this time, I had to salvage from the waters what remained of my fairy tales, in the same way that fishermen pull from the deep water sprites or mermaids, creatures whose existence they had doubted right up until the moment they caught them.

It was pouring with rain as Nhean accompanied me to the bus station where, only a week earlier, he had recruited me as a passenger on a boat trip across the Tonle Sap to Siem Reap and Angkor. As we said goodbye, we exchanged addresses on the world-wide web, but neither of us truly believed that we would ever see the other again.

The crush or wrangle among the buses was a reminder that here as well, in this part of the world, too many people were engaged in a battle for shelter, work and food to be able to forge lasting friendships, communities and relationships. Emblazoned in red lettering on the black background of Nhean's faded, hole-riddled T-shirt was a law written in the Khmer language that the boatman translated for me as *Everyone for himself*. It was not until an embarrassed moment during our farewells, casting around in vain for something fitting to say, that I asked him what the red symbols on his chest meant.

Boarding the bus to the Laotian border and Nakasong, I got into an argument with a wiry, bald tourist from the North American Alliance over my reserved seat in this vehicle packed with passengers, few of whom were less soaked than me, their clothes stinking and steaming. The man would not listen, repeating again and again that he had been on the bus long before me, and I was about to yank him out of the seat by his tattooed arm when a uniformed conductor informed the wiry man that he should refill and replant the bomb craters America had blown in villages, cities, paddy fields and plantations over the centuries before travelling through Cambodia and pushed him out of the bus to surreptitious sniggers from several passengers.

It took us over 11 hours to reach the port 10 miles beyond the Cambodian border from where a ferry could take me to the islands. There, just as Mira and I had planned, I boarded a boat to the Laotian river island of Don Khong. It had been Mira who had chosen Don Khong as the jumping-off point for our trip. Not until I was making for the landing stage where they only accepted the national currency for the rental kayaks—here too, the lustre and value of the dollar had faded—and a woman lowered her bright-yellow parasol and looked at me with amazement and possibly a hint of amusement, did I realize that I must have been talking about and cursing Mira all the way from the bus to the jetty. The dyke reeve's wife had left me in the lurch, in the downpours of those days. But this monologue was merely the beginning of a long dispute involving not just my invisible sister but also my mother Jana, who had gone missing on the Adriatic island of her birth, and my father, the fugitive murderer.

Until then, I had only ever held these soliloquies against the backdrop of the roaring Great Falls, when I used the water music that drowned out my words as cover and a filter not only to whisper otherwise unspeakable words but also to scream curses, swearwords and obscenities that alleviated whatever happened to be weighing on my mind at the spray, the rocks or the clouds. As counterweights.

The owner of a dozen neon-coloured kayaks, with whom I had eventually agreed a week-long rental price for a sky-blue boat bearing some deep notches and the scratches of impacts on its hull, told me of a feud between two island villages triggered by a boat race one had narrowly won and the other narrowly lost. This battle had claimed three lives, and even before I climbed into my boat, armed with insistent warnings and route recommendations, a connection was taking shape between the European regions and water-poor battlefields all around Bandon and the island kingdom through which I was planning to travel. One law obviously governed the two places, here and there, and Nhean wore it in red letters across his chest: *Everyone for himself.* The four thousand islands pounded by the waters of the Mekong suddenly seemed a model of the future of a European continent enmeshed in high-voltage cables, rivers, rail lines and border fences.

Here and there, the torrent and deafness and blindness towards anything that was unknown and anything foreign pounded the islands and reserves into ever-smaller pieces until eventually all that would be left, standing in the wilderness, would be jetty-less boat people, unyielding patriots and stragglers, while fishermen, lockkeepers and flag-wavers attacked and butchered one another in alleged defence of their landing and angling sites, their traditional costumes, customs and languages.

Was this how Mira and I had imagined the paradise or currents and islands? Every shore was thick with vegetation and as flat as a raft; the eddies, the smooth current and the whirlpools around the sandbanks really did resemble the images in our dreams. And yet Mira was far away—shockingly far away. She had broken her promise, which throughout the past months had always been my bright sliver of hope in the grey overcast sky of the monsoon days as I worked on relief channels, reservoirs and dams on de-mined rice fields. She had gone missing like Jana, run away like my father. Unreachable.

But in the engine noise of ferries, fishing boats and lorries and in the rustling of the teak forests I heard her voice. In the rippling waves of the Mekong, I saw her picking strawberries and felt the firm grip with which, despite her brittle bones, she had wrenched from me the scissors I was using to cut in half the zigzagging hornets near the lockmaster's house. I could recite long passages from the stories she had read aloud to me. I heard her laughter. And her stomach warmed my forehead. Her fingertips skipped and ran, glided and hurried over every hollow and every plain on my body, every nook and cranny, traced my lips and forced their way through thickets of hair, encountering no resistance. I wasn't a pharaoh. I was just a water carrier for the builders of a pyramid made of memory, longing, disappointment and anger.

My route for the first few days of my kayak trip on the Mekong was quite like the flightpath of a hornet or a housefly—a tangle of constantly changing directions and objectives. Current allowing, I drifted this way and that on the smooth water before once more resisting the current with furious strokes of my paddle or surrendering to the attraction of a distant, alluring goal upstream or a mysterious, shimmering cloud over the dark-green riverside thickets, which turned out, on closer inspection, to be a flock of white ibises that scattered like an explosion at the sound of my paddle. I approached the skeleton of a drowned giant, which metamorphosed first into a whale carcass and finally into the mossy wreck of a longboat caught in curtains of lianas in shallow water by a sandbank. As night fell, I paddled towards the lights of a riverside village which turned into a barricade of black, phosphorescent driftwood.

Once, I was so scared by inexplicable noises along a pitch-black stretch of bank—I couldn't tell whether the screeching and shrill cries came from humans or animals—that I tied my boat to the starward-probing aerial roots of a banyan tree felled by flooding, and slept in the kayak in a grotesque position until cramp woke me and I drifted downstream at first light in search of a more comfortable place to lie down and rest.

However, with every loop around one of the islands, the more familiar the stretch of river from Si Phan Don became during my days on the water, the more this knotty route unravelled and began to resemble the voyages of exploration that had led Mira and me through the universe to the stars. We may have sailed through dimensions of space and time only via the screens in the lockmaster's house, but those hours had taken us farther from the Great Falls than any inhabitant of the banks of the White River had ever gone.

We had been led to the edges of our universe—without ever needing to fear rebuke from Jana or my father—by constantly updated computer programs of ever more mind-blowing complexity devoted to reaching and conquering black holes, giant suns many light years away and tracts of malevolent sky, crisscrossed by hostile fleets. We had subjugated or destroyed planetary systems and, whenever we went outdoors, we had woven the patterns of intergalactic games over cliffs, rocky shores and sandbanks in order to carry on spinning our fictions on the banks of the White River and in the spray of the Great Falls. Dippers became harbingers of incoming aliens, rainbow trout and perch were lightning-fast messengers from nameless civilizations, and the caves hollowed out by the current became gravitational holes that swallowed everything the White River and its lethal force carried into their maws.

Mira, my pharaoh queen, had orbited dying suns with me, baptized spectral residents of ice planets and given them backstories until we could no longer find new things to name, destroy or conquer and held each other silently and wearily by the hand.

It was as if memories of these games were dredged up by my paddle strokes from the depths of the Mekong and rained down on my route like a shower of droplets, and sometimes I really did drift through those days with the pharaoh queen. Not just her, either. I shouted questions to my mother, Jana, and curses at my father over the water's symphonic sounds, but the Mekong offered up no intelligible answers. I'm the son of a murderer, my mother heard me scream over and over again; and I threatened her missing husband: I will look for you. I will find you. I will kill you. And on the racing Mekong murmured. And on I raced on the murmuring Mekong.

Every island I circled was an undiscovered planet. The currents that tugged at my vessel, thrusting it towards whirlpools into which you would vanish for ever if you didn't paddle with all your might, were filled with asteroid showers, the wrecks of space cruisers and comets knocked off their orbits.

And when, far out in space, light years out, I was finally all alone, the banks were gradually populated with the inhabitants of Bandon, wearing conical hats and standing up to their knees, not in paddy fields but in flooded strawberry fields that stained the water red. Red as blood. Those who had drowned in the White River picked the sweet fruit to the sound of piano playing and the arias of the phantom catwoman, her voice echoing inside my head. A turbine warden stretched out his arms in vain to the clouds, trying to climb the steps of a cumulus that towered up into the stratosphere. And a seamstress tumbled through the rapids in her gold-embroidered traditional costume while her deaf daughter burbled cries for help at the thundering current.

So I dipped my paddle into time and steered my kayak every way it flowed without ever reaching the present. I was the son of a man who had hauled himself through his whole life in the shadow of the past, who had been willing to kill in order to stay in this dark realm. And who had trapped me in the memory of a deed that I knew only from eyewitness reports and that had therefore taken on a nebulous form in my head and become an all-pervasive presence.

I will look for you, I shouted above the water, dug my paddle into the waves and saw the people bending over the mirroring paddy fields on the banks raise their conical-hatted heads and track my progress with their eyes. I will look for you. I will kill you.

When, after nine days on the river, I reached the port of Veun Kham on the Cambodian–Laotian border and found a connection to the Great Net on a landing stage lit with fairy lights and, in a windowless bamboo hut flickering with screens, a keyboard that used my alphabet, I untied the kayak and let it float away downstream, empty. It would carry my unfulfilled longing for embraces, tenderness and Egyptian love, so inextricably entwined with Mira, to the South China Sea. Via the Net I sent the boat's owner money and a message that his kayak had been lost in the cataracts of Khone Phapheng. Without responding to his angry reply, I and nine other passengers (five of them employed, like me, by the syndicate) set off in a freezing air-conditioned minibus for my water construction sites in the Cambodian interior.

As if not just the Khmers but all visitors to the country needed constant reminders of the cataclysm induced by the glorification of a supposedly triumphant past peopled with gods, Nibelungen or classical war heroes, the bus passed three of the skull towers dotted all over the country that displayed, between concrete columns and glass walls, the remains of the victims of the violent Khmer Blanc regime.

I had often encountered such memorials while travelling to my construction sites, but this time I sensed, as never before, that these towers were signposts to the abysses of my own life. For many centuries after their construction, the temples of imperial Angkor had pointed the way to a fresh descent into barbarism in similar fashion to the sluice gates and boat channels and other structures that helped to circumvent the Great Falls, built by the lockmasters—those masters of life and death, whom my father had been so desperate to emulate.

But what had succumbed to the course of time was not reinstated at the Great Falls either. Even rivers capable of reversing their flow and returning to their sources merely served as a reminder that it was, at best, for the gods who governed the alternation of dry and rainy seasons to decide what they could do, but never for humans.

Should mortals still be tempted to reverse the course of time and rekindle the ashes of glory in breach of all the laws of time, they mutated into murderers. Even terms of endearment turned to curses or even death sentences then—and water turned to blood.

SEVEN

Humiliation

I was informed of the *Rotterdam Sanctions* by an encrypted file
that had lain waiting for me for several days in a special inbox file
set up by the Cambodian water authority on the Sen river. Files
like this—orders and instructions from the syndicate—could only
be consulted via the quantum computer in Kampong Thom and
were stored in a tamper-proof archive after reading. Any attempt
to transfer messages or the syndicate's structural plans at any public
Net station to a mobile computer unfailingly generated an empty,
white screen, which went black after precisely nine seconds and
subsequently blocked the accessing device for several days, or,
depending on the sensitivity of the data, displayed a signal of per-
manent exclusion from the Net, thus relegating a mobile reception
device to a piece of junk.

Rotterdam, the city where I had passed my examinations and
obtained my hydraulic-engineering degree, had withdrawn from
one of the four North Atlantic Alliances and declared its harbour—
which, despite competition from Antwerp, was still the largest sea
port on the European continent—an independent city-state.

The city's former allies, who had been demoted to mere customers at the docks by what separatists hailed as a *revolutionary step*—although, in fact, it merely accelerated the nationalist-fuelled process of European shrinkage—had, after a series of bloody clashes between the Rotterdam rebels and the Rhone–Meuse Alliance, imposed a series of sanctions with ramifications even for the omnipotent intercontinental syndicate to whom I had been answerable since graduating. All teaching staff educated at one of Rotterdam's universities or hydraulic-engineering institutes, who had hitherto been appointed and controlled by the Alliance, were withdrawn. All qualifications awarded by these scientific and technical institutions were declared null and void. Anyone entrusted with a job or holding a water office by virtue of their Rotterdam diploma was forced to prove their aptitude by sitting for a series of relevant exams and serving unpaid probation periods ranging from a few months to two years.

Even the University of Rotterdam, until recently the centre of the continent's hydraulic engineering, lost its pre-eminent status. In the final analysis, the North Sea offered alternative access points to the global water trade which had long since replaced former state structures with a network spanning the continents, rivers and oceans and a power system that tolerated no criticism.

For me these sanctions would have meant that I was now dependent on bodies and authorities to whose lower-ranking staff, now the beneficiaries of nepotism, I—I!—had previously given orders. Idiots of the class of a dyke reeve or even a clueless technician in the licensing authority for small power plants and vortex power plants could now drive innovators and development engineers like me—people who had built these kinds of plants and raised them to previously unimaginable levels of efficiency—mad with their certificates, reprimands and instructions.

Despite having no idea which area of hydraulic engineering I might change to—after all, there was barely a water course anywhere that slipped through the syndicate's net on its way to the sea—I immediately handed in my notice.

In all my years working for the syndicate in the world's major catchment areas, I had not once seen the face of a superior or a project manager or ever heard a human voice from the upper echelons of the organization, even when reception was excellent; every time I had to ask, clarify or assess something, I had read anonymous, codenamed notifications on my screen. It was entirely possible that behind the reams of correspondence between myself and the syndicate lay nothing but an algorithm that could scrape details from the global flow of data and liberally combine them, thereby ensuring its own long-term survival free from human intervention.

Which is why it was a puzzling and, yes, humiliating surprise, while I was still at the Sen river, to have my resignation greeted with an immediate reply that might have been created by software but hit me with the force of a curse. Rather than being sent on intercontinental missions, I was to take over the memorial campus on the White River—the museum-like sluice gates and boat channels around the Great Falls! The notification stated that this required no hydrology qualifications and, who knows, once the current turbulence had died down, maybe I could work my way back up from this position to my former level in the hierarchy. If I accepted this offer, I would be granted three months' paid transitional leave before taking up my new functions at the Great Falls.

I would have left this imposed humiliation unanswered and approved its deletion as I sat in a tea house on the banks of the Sen river, downing a shot of rice brandy with every bowl of tea, had I not seen this offer—three months' unpaid transitional leave with no prescribed assignments—as a magnetic prospect.

As my brandy-induced fogginess thickened by the Sen river, I contemplated applying to be a legionnaire for an alliance of Andalusian villages, towns and clans battling over three river springs and disputed water rights in the Sierra Nevada. Yet each additional glass increasingly convinced me of the advantages of the syndicate's offer: While on gardening leave, I could perhaps pick up my sister's trail and my father's too. And I might even be able to turn Jana back from a simple image in my memory and an imaginary figure into a speaking, breathing person.

The last news I had received of Jana was a blurred digital picture of a village of huddled stone houses on the cliffs of the Adriatic island of Cres, which had appeared on my phone display over two years earlier. Perhaps if she had written to me on my construction projects, her messages had fallen victim to the censorship filters designed to prevent trouble breaking out at our assignment sites and, above all, in the minds of the technical staff. That two-year-old message under the picture of a stone village had stated that the authorities had approved her irreversible separation from our father. She wrote that she was finally free.

Although I doubted that three months would be sufficient for the many applications and authorizations, route permits, visas, passports, epidemic tests and health certificates I required to travel to the North Sea and later to the Adriatic given that my travels served no technical purpose, my plans were set by the time I embarked on the syndicate's twin-engine transport plane in Phnom Penh. I would use the three remaining months before I started my spell as a lockmaster to look for the real, vanished people of my past and force them to tell me why they had disappeared from my life. And I would move into the house I had grown up in beside the Great Falls once I had found an answer to the question of why I should now be its sole occupant.

The flight corridors binding Asia and Europe together were no less fragmented than the routes on the European continent, compelling every aircraft moving between the shifting Siberian, Russian and Chinese spheres of dominance to undergo a sequence of transit checks, form-filling exercises and transfer procedures. Flights that used to take little more than 10 or 12 hours in *more blessed times*, as one of the co-pilots said in his moody welcome announcement, now lasted for five days or more.

When I had weathered a purgatory of queues, questioning and sleepless nights in transit areas and finally boarded the train, whose doors were sealed prior to departure, connecting the major airport in the former protectorate of Birkenau-North to commissariats and counties in the Alpine foothills, I felt so downcast and tired that an officer of the heavily armed, black-uniformed security team had to wake me from a dreamless sleep and alert me to the fact that the ticket loaded into my armband was chirping shrilly.

It was high time to change onto the *Transcontinental* to the conflict zones on the Elbe estuary, another digitally locked train that would take me without stopping to the North Sea and to Mira. She had either not received any of my announcements due to one of the many *updates* to the censorship laws, or had filtered them out of her inbox herself as undesirable.

Virtually every explanation I concocted to explain her silence enraged me, but a two- or three-day journey that crossed twenty or more borders was bound to lift the fog of helplessness in my mind. Whenever I dozed off during my travels, still exhausted from the time differences, I felt, amid my crazy, numbing daydreams, something like hope that there might actually be a comforting reason I hadn't considered for the silence between Mira and me that would dispel my anger when I reached my destination.

Snow.

Snow. It had been years since I had last seen snow, then I woke—after sleeping through only two hours of my journey in the lounge car reserved for hydraulic engineers of a presumably once-gleaming silver Transcontinental now dotted with patches of rust—to . . . snow. The fields and occasional scattered bastions and watchtowers flashing past the tinted windows of the compartment I shared with three other taciturn hydrologists were weighed down by a layer of snow that seemed to thicken with every second in the swirling, driving, white blizzard. Hadn't all predictions about climate change evoked images of Mediterranean or even subtropical scenery in these latitudes, foreseen palm trees swaying by the Elbe and rhododendrons and bougainvillea flowering here?

In the compartment, the only suggestion of tropical climes was the leopard-skin hat that one of my travel companions was wearing. This hat was the insignia of an engineer with permission to adorn himself in the aristocratic raiment of each region he worked in. What an idiot. It would never have occurred to me to fasten a crown of feathers I had bought in the Amazon around my head.

The silent leopard opposite me, absorbed in studying maps, and not once removing his sunglasses, even though the landscape was bathed in grey wintry light, had clearly done his duty by the Victoria Falls. I had read a lot about the fighting that had flared up along the Zambezi over dam projects and the resulting submergence of whole districts, hunting lands and villages. The military cost of these uprisings had bankrupted a Texan syndicate. A hydro-syndicate, bankrupt! A unique case in the apparently invincible ranks of the global water industry.

During my time on the Rio Xingu and even more so later on, among the mined paddy fields on the banks of the Mekong, I had secretly imagined that the warming of the terrestrial climate might have made the vegetation of the landscape of my childhood and perhaps even the North Atlantic wastelands around Mira's new home no longer too dissimilar to the verdant Asian scenery. I clearly remembered from my last visit to the Great Falls that marsh lilies and orchids I had never seen before were in bloom. But now: snow. Snow, whose on–off gleam (the sun piercing through slits in the clouds was almost painful) carried me, as I dozed in my train compartment, back to my childhood winters by the White River.

Back then, pillars of ice as thick as trees had welded the sky to eddies grown sluggish with the low flow over the Great Falls. *Heavenly palaces*, Mira had called the frosted glassy structures rearing out of the remaining water that trickled from the steep steps of the falls, the reflected sunlight twinkling in their crystalline texture like a hail of sparks.

Mira. I saw every image as clearly and coldly as one of the corymbs of heady-scented viburnum bushes, sprayed and frozen with water from the gutter, which flowered in the shadow of the lockmaster's house during the Christmas period and even when the cold had turned everything to glass. Jana had planted these shrubs in memory of her Adriatic homeland, towering bushes that shed their leaves in the autumn and produced clusters of inflorescence smelling of lilac and violets on the tips of their bare branches, as if their airiness were celebrating some kind of triumph over the frost and the snow.

Each time the Transcontinental stopped in the middle of nowhere for an hour or more, generally in darkness, the fingers of light from laser devices wielded by checkpoint guards crept across the carriage's windows and doors sealed with bars bearing the passengers' data, photos, visas and travel permits. As far as I could tell, only twice before the terminus at the mouth of the Elbe were one carriage's digital seals unlocked and suspects dragged off to a waiting armoured personnel carrier. The hydraulic engineers sharing my compartment watched the ballet of indistinct figures in the darkness in the same silence and with the same apparent indifference as I did. It could be dangerous to comment on incidents of this nature in front of strangers because this train was directed from a distant headquarters and had eyes and ears like any of the other transport infrastructure that various tribes, commissariats and clans operated jointly in their only concession to multilateral interests. What was seen through carelessly camouflaged lenses and heard through equally carelessly camouflaged microphones— why the camouflage when ubiquitous surveillance was a standard feature of public space?—could cause the train to stop between stations and armoured vehicles to arrive and chase ghostly figures through the darkness.

On the morning of the third day of my journey to the northern Atlantic, when the snow blanket covering the land had thinned with every passing mile and gradually melted away into the mud of the treeless, bushless pastures, the marine horizon drew a steel-grey line across the compartment window. It was impossible to tell whether what the passengers saw in the distance was indeed the sea or just the wave-marked mudflats reflecting the sky, as if the sandy sea bottom had been levered up out of the deep and lacquered by the receding water.

I had reached my destination. However, the terminus, announced by a flowing ribbon of red text, lay in the midst of an emptiness that fanned out in every direction—nothing but sky, nothing but water and silt and sand, spanned only by seemingly endless bridge structures connecting an invisible mainland far beyond the horizon to the ocean. The main station loomed up out the waves like one of the old Atlantic drilling rigs from some long-lost century atop a colonnade of steel pylons, as if it were stretching out seven, eight, nine or more spidery arms towards the mainland but their only purchase was on a horizon of silt and water. Docked against the buffers in the spider's belly were several trains guarded by people in black uniforms—the spider's prey, wrapped in a film of condensation.

The doors of the Transcontinental did not open until armed station staff in combat gear indistinguishable from that of a fighting force had checked the passengers' names and ticket numbers and the results had been projected onto a flickering screen above the buffers.

I had seen the steel connecting bridges arcing over many square miles of flooded land before on a travel-agency photo that Mira had sent me in the Amazon. In it, the spider was reaching for a cloud that obscured the sky—censorship software had clearly blacked out part of the image of the central railway station to prevent anyone identifying the edifice's strategic or architectural features.

As if strings of satellites and the bombing squadrons involved in the Friesland Wars that had flared up again in recent months could not highlight every detail of bridges and railway embankments on their target with far greater precision than a postcard might. What a strange attitude, an approach reminiscent of now-inconceivable air battles. Using the keycodes that were my privilege as a hydraulic engineer, even I could sift the coordinates of the station from the Net. But maybe this censorship was aimed not at the spider or the central railway station but at the occasional vestiges that protruded—even if they were sometimes only visible at second glance—from the waters of tidal creeks and navigation channels as the last reminders of the dykes, villages, streets and even towers submerged by the rising sea level.

What was displayed here, as if in mockery, was something that was otherwise found only in pictures of the dam walls of the newest run-of-the-river power stations: water that rose and rose until eventually it got the upper hand and buried everything beneath it. The sea—this was what the grey waterworld's submergence of all the land around the central railway station demonstrated—the sea could also do this: it could reclaim all the things it had once released in countless shapes and forms onto dry land. Anything that had climbed out of the deep aeons ago and begun to rampage along the shorelines was bound, at some stage, to return to the deep. Sooner or later, all land would revert to being as barren and empty as at the dawn of time, under a sky occluded by clouds of steam.

When I emerged from the glass-roofed arrivals hall into the open air after baggage checks that were long even for privileged travellers like myself, I confused the roar of the rising waters in the steel pylons with the thunder of the Great Falls. I stood there under a steel-grey sky arcing over the steel-grey sea of Mira's new world like a shapeless, formless fog, and I heard the thunder of the Great Falls.

Even though I didn't know whether my sister had received the news of my demotion to lockmaster and my plan to travel to the Atlantic to be close to her (I had also sent her the identification numbers of my passenger permits), I had made no arrangements to stay on a coast monitored by hundreds of measuring devices as, with every passing day, it retreated further before the waves. Where some accommodation or at least a dry shelter had stood only a year earlier, the sea now roared, shrinking the tasks of hydraulic engineers to emergency defence—their core job along the coasts of an ocean that had long since started to raise its surface, swollen by melting polar icecaps, higher and higher into the sky, was no longer to store and channel water and lead it to the turbines, but to banish it like a biblical plague.

No hotels. No rooms with views. No accommodation. I had assumed that it must be possible to track down a dyke reeve's residence, Mira's home, despite all the security measures shielding these residences from normal life. A tower! Mira had written excitedly to me by the Rio Xingu long ago—a lighthouse ringed with the remains of sunken dyke buildings that looked like curtain walls. But all I could see in every direction was the sea.

The breakers pounding away among the pillars and the wind howling in the pylons rendered inaudible the hubbub of voices outside the station's main portal. Hundreds of people were jostling to meet the new arrivals. Signs with names of places and clans were brandished, banners reading *Welcome to the waves!* were held aloft, along with others saying *Get back in your holes, you land rats!*

When a hand suddenly clenched my shoulder in the middle of this chaos and did not release its grip and I started to turn around, I was prepared to undergo another check by one of the many people in uniform. But I hesitantly kept on going—and slowly turned into Mira's embrace, into the arms of my glass girl.

She was smiling, as if in all those months and years of being at a silent distance from me, she had been waiting for me—me alone. Yet when I tried to respond to her embrace and hold her tight, as cautiously as ever so as not to damage her delicate ribcage, her fine vertebrae and brittle joints, I felt metal in the way of this intimacy.

Mira was wearing one of those nickel-plated automatic weapons resembling imperial silverwork, which, in Bandon county at least, no one but syndicate officers and high-ranking members of the security forces was allowed to bear.

We're at war, she whispered, eluding my attempted kiss.

At war? With me? I said, resting my hand on the gun barrel which was wet with swirling flakes of spray or rain.

At war with the sea, she continued in a whisper, even though no one could possibly have heard us over the chorus of many voices and waves smashing against the pillars; at war with the sea and people's lust for dry land.

EIGHT

Killing

Mira, my girl of glass. My glass sister. What a woman. She looked every bit as desirable as in the feverish dreams that had disturbed my nights at the construction camps along the Mekong and the Amazon. The dyke reeve—her companion, her possessor!—whom I hated because he had abducted her, had been missing for weeks from the conning towers where he was fighting a minor war over dams and discharge systems. Even Mira received only contradictory reports of these skirmishes. Some sections of the frontline along the North Sea resembled the tracks of wild animals, moving this way one day and that the next, repeatedly scything through paths and lines of communication and leaving nothing but a mire pitted with graves and trenches and battlefields flooded with brackish water.

The hulking round tower of granite and red brick in which my sister showed me to my guest quarters was familiar from flash-lit photographs she had attached to her transatlantic messages. The walls of the room were decorated with albatrosses and herring gulls painted in the texture of a sailor's tattoo onto the plaster. The floor was carpeted with seal skins, and the duvet was filled with the down of eider ducks. And yet the room kept none of the promises of my dreams. No rest. No peace and quiet. No safety in Mira's embrace. Even if I burrowed like a blind newborn mammal into the seal skins that covered the floorboards crafted from the hull of a boat and completely muffled any footsteps, still the North Sea roared in my ears.

Yes! Yes, of course, Mira had received all my messages, including the ones about the day and time of my arrival. But had her replies really been absorbed by the syndicate's filters or the electronic firewalls of the coastal authorities, as she suspected?

Anyway, she had been waiting for me at the appointed time and taken me from the central railway station in a boat belonging to the dyke reeve's office. The trip along channels and creeks that switched direction according to the incoming and ebbing water had reminded me of those outings at our father's side when every word had died in the din of the water and the engine. The only means of making instructions, questions and answers intelligible had been to shout them.

If you weren't familiar with the currents that changed to the cycle of the tides, Mira had yelled to me over the engine noise, then after an odyssey of many hours you might find yourself not at your destination but somewhere far over the horizon, far out, far beyond hope of rescue. There was fighting over these channels and these creeks too, she cried; a gun was as essential as a navigation aid and a lifejacket in these waters, just in case you crossed the frontline.

I don't have either, I shouted to Mira. And I laughed. I had never held any weapon other than a knife. She merely pointed to an aluminium box next to my seat.

During our passage, the boat ploughed through a grey swell produced by unpredictable cross waves. I could detect no troop positions or signs of combat anywhere.

Those who controlled the waterways leading to a particular place, Mira said after cutting the engines at the lighthouse quay and stowing her gun in a water-stained sling bag, would soon control those places too, the ports and the dry land. The price of every sandbank that emerged from the waters as a pale crescent today and was gone again tomorrow or had reappeared elsewhere was paid for in dead bodies. Even the most fleeting possession of land lost or regained with the back and forth of the tides was precious. After all—and this was probably no different in the southern interior?—chiefs were fighting over a ludicrously narrow coastline or a toy-sized county not just for more or less territory but for their very existence. What the vanquished in a war of pygmies lost was not grandeur; the blows of its enemy reduced it to nothingness, from which there was virtually no hope of return. How could a pygmy who had been driven into invisibility and insignificance muster the energy to return to being an entity worthy of mention?

There were 50 stone steps up from the quay to my tower room. The windows were portholes staring out in every direction, and every hole—apart from a north-facing one where the distant steel spider crouched, arms outstretched towards the black coastline, beneath a steel-grey bank of clouds—framed only water.

Churned-up, surf-topped saltwater, billowing by the gusty wind into chaotic commotion.

Like a castaway, I had said to Mira as we climbed up to the storm-proof lighthouse entrance from the quayside protected by breakwaters of reinforced-concrete cubes, you live like a castaway on a rock in the sea.

You can cross the mudflats to the shore quickly at low tide in your boots, she said. Me, a castaway? You were washed up in the deltas of the world's great rivers; I followed the course of the White River. Even the Great Falls rushes towards the ocean. Sooner or later, everyone reaches the open sea.

Mira. How long had it been since we had last seen each other? I had stopped counting the months long ago. There had been times when I had known the number of days, even hours that had passed since our most recent farewell. How I would have liked to take her in my arms as she showed me my quarters redolent with the tobacco and brandy of the sailors who had supplied the lighthouse with provisions while it still towered above a peninsula overgrown with gorse, lyme grass and heather, not just grey water, nothing but water, whatever the height of the tide. However, I did not want to experience the humiliation of Mira recoiling from me again so soon after she had rejected my embrace on the platform.

Ever since she had burst out of the calm water of the White River in a cloud of spray and swum towards me and taken me in her arms, each of our encounters had been a repeat of that first, overpowering event. Whenever and wherever we subsequently came into contact—*she* had always been one step ahead of me, leading me. When I dreamt of those moments, even hours after waking, the line between reality and pure fantasy was still unclear.

I may not have felt any more painful disappointment in life than in that instant under the steel structure of the station canopy when she dodged my attempt to hug her. A pharaoh rejected! It was as if even my heartbeat had suddenly slowed, and my blood wasn't coursing and pulsating through my arteries as it otherwise did when we were reunited but oozed through them instead, sluggish and hot, on the verge of standstill.

What is it? Mira had asked, looking at me with concern as if something trivial had just happened. What's wrong with you? You've gone as white as our river.

Even in my daydreams and conflicting recollections, I return again and again to that moment and wonder what might have been had I made a more decisive attempt to reconnect with our previous affectionate closeness and confessed how unbearable I found the chasm between my desires and the reality beneath that sky of steel. Might the drama of our reunion after such a long time have taken a different path before her—and our—fateful demise? Would what eventually happened never have happened?

But I didn't say a word at the time and did nothing to reveal my true feelings to Mira, my lust for her skin and her frail body, my hatred for the man who seemed to rule her life. All I said was: How cold it is on your coast. I'm cold.

There is no coast here, my girl of glass said. Only sea.

In the first of the total of nine days I spent in the lighthouse, I hoped every night that Mira, who slept two storeys above me in the *Turret* under the beacon—as inaccessible as the canopy of a gigantic first-growth tree—would slip into my room in the middle of the night. That was how it had been in our parents' house by the White River, and the Great Falls had then drowned out every one of our gasps, every sound of our desire. Here, it would have been the ocean itself that embedded any noise in the reverberating thunder of the world, heard by us alone. Not once in those nights did Mira come down from her eyrie into my seal-skin room, however, and I did not mention the matter during our breakfasts in a circular parlour decorated with wave mosaics. And nor did she.

We were indeed the lockmaster's children. We may not have been trapped in a supposedly glorious, superior past as he was, but we were bewitched by the magic of the memories of our days as pharaoh and pharaoh queen, excited children between moss-covered towers of rock, on the sandbanks and by the cataracts of the White River, our very own Nile—a playground ringed by fiery orange lilies where we had been convinced that Moses had been washed ashore as a crying infant in a wickerwork basket and rescued by one of the pharaoh queen's maids.

Maybe, in fact, I alone had succumbed to this magic, and Mira's willingness to advance with me into the river landscapes of the past was the one and only loving favour she could do for me. Sometimes she would even jolt my memory with forgotten details and readily agreed with me that the sound of the Atlantic breakers was the roar of the Great Falls. Flakes of spray swirling around the tower became the snow above the catwoman's strawberry fields in Bandon. One day in May, while the catwoman sang her arias and her audience was trying to pick as much as possible as a storm brewed, it had indeed snowed so heavily that the ripe berries glowed like gobs of blood against the wet white of the spring snow. The catwoman had gone on singing, not even bothering to shut her windows against the snow flurries, as her audience, which included Mira and me, wandered around in the blizzard with hands and mouths full of cold strawberries.

Mira. Had she really found happiness without me, without her pharaoh, and had she followed a water warrior's shock of blue hair to the North Sea not through calculation or an iron determination to raise her status within the waterworld by being by his bride, but for love? Would my days in that damned lighthouse have in any case been *final* days, as irreversible as the flight of a pebble hurled into the ceaseless cascades of the Great Falls?

On our long excursions in her blue-maned husband's powerboat, which Mira manoeuvred no less expertly than our father had steered his motorized lighter along the White River, we landed on sandbanks thick with harbour seals and grey seals and cooked the fish we had caught on the way amid razed farms on dykeless islands, advanced outposts abandoned years ago by a society retreating from the ocean.

As Mira's passenger on ever-longer excursions into a waterworld of which she seemed so proud that she wanted to show me every particularity of the shoreline despite the risk of venturing into conflict zones, I was eventually forced to admit to myself that it was mainly me, and me alone, who screamed memories at the pounding waves, the noise of the engine and against the wind in an attempt to bring the pharaoh queen back to life, like a mummy in its sarcophagus. The naked beauty rising from the clear waters of Mesopotamia must be resurrected and join me on my path to happiness.

Mira listened to me, smiling occasionally as I invoked the past, but mostly she said nothing

Are you . . . I wrote for her with the boat hook on a seal-colonized sandbank to which we had been lured by the wailing of an abandoned baby seal . . . Have you stopped being a pharaoh queen and become a sphinx?

Mira sank to her knees in the clumpy sand and traced her answer with her index finger among the washed-up remains of a spider crab: I've never been to the Nile.

Sitting a mere arm's length from our sand inscriptions and yet unimaginably far from each other in the late-afternoon sun, we watched the baby seal slide back into the water with its suddenly surfacing mother, which seemed unsure whether she should attack Mira and me as a threat to her young or suckle her offspring. Within minutes, the incoming tide had reached our writing and erased it. It was now windy and cold. Despite its twin engines, the boat struggled against the current and it took us over an hour to make it back to the lighthouse.

In the following days, it was mainly sands—elongated seal shoals or silt barriers strewn with rubble and rubbish, the vestiges of beachings and shipwrecks—that determined the routes of our outings, either as their destinations or simply as island landmarks.

As in our kayaks on the White River, where Mira had shown me the invisible navigable routes running between shallows, rocky underwater ledges and eddies, here it was the confused channels coursing along the countless creeks, shifting with the rising and falling tide and slithering through sand and between shoals, like some glassy, snake-like deep-sea creature pressing its way towards the light.

Mira followed every curve of this creature, often laughing, and brought us to beaches on so many banks and islets whose names and histories I more frequently read on her lips than I actually heard them as we raced loudly up the steep inclines to the crests of the waves.

It was on one of these outings that I realized for the first time that the many different sounds water made—the thundering of the Great Falls, the roar of the surf or a simple downpour—often filled my head to such an extent that anything that wasn't part of that water—not a river large or small, the sea or even a windswept lake—lost clarity and sometimes became inaudible.

Amid the raging of the Great Falls, while opening a sluice or the floodgates of a dam across one of the great rivers, I had learnt to communicate in sign language and to understand orders by lip-reading. It was, however, only over the course of these days that I began to comprehend that I bore the roaring of the water inside me and that sometimes, even when I was a long way from any flowing or standing water, I couldn't catch what someone was saying or calling to me.

While Mira was steering the boat from the dyke reeve's office through shallows and shifting currents far out at sea, as if she had an infallible chart of this branching shoreline imprinted on her memory, her voice also grew fainter and fainter and faded away to nothing. At the same time, ineluctable memories came bubbling up out of the most remote regions of my waterworld—memories of the White River, snow falling in Bandon, the arias of a drowned teacher and the severed halves of wasps and hornets tumbling out of the blue summer sky.

I barely noticed that I reacted to the quietening, indeed the extinguishing of Mira's voice not with increased alertness and concentration but by staring at her like someone instinctively searching for a modulator, a switch, some mechanical aid to restore the dimming, diminishing sound to an audible level. But there was no such aid, no such switch. Not on the Atlantic coast nor on the banks of any of the world's rivers.

When I had to check with Mira three times before I finally got the name, after she had called out to me that our next destination was a seal island marked on maritime charts as *Amber Bank*, I realized when she cried *Are you deaf?* that I had stopped trying to understand her acoustically but had attempted to read her lips as I used to amid the booming of the Great Falls.

KILLING

It was only long after my escape from the lighthouse that I noticed that the roar of the water in my head and in my heart deafened me only when I lingered, either physically or in my thoughts and daydreams, on riverbanks or coasts or in the pouring rain. On firm, dry land or in the interior of a country or in the deserts that had replaced countryside where carpets of crops once swayed, the singing and rushing and whispering of water abated—unless a memory drew me back to a shore or beach. Voices and even birdsong and the chirping and buzzing of insects would then detach themselves from the water noise like sparks from a flame—gone. And the world fell silent.

Too late I realized that on this embattled stretch of coastline in the north of a simultaneously sinking *and* parching continent, what Mira had found was not so much love as the greatest possible distance from the Great Falls, from the lives of our parents, particularly her past-obsessed father, and perhaps also from her brother who still fantasized about her by day. She would do anything not to go back there, ever. But *there* also meant *me*. I came from *there*, dragging along images of the water meadows along the White River like a decor, and it seemed that I would be no less of a captive of the Bandon gorge than our father had been. Or still was?

He was alive?

No, Mira was convinced that our father had vanished for ever at the Great Falls and certainly not staged his disappearance witnessed by a fly-fisherman. Also, when I told her about the clay hand—my find in the Mesopotamian silt—she refused to see it as evidence of a faked drowning but simply as proof of my

111

determination to look for a scapegoat for the tarnishing of the memories of our life by the falls.

On her way to the North Sea, Mira seemed to have shed—like a snake sheds its skin—the world I not only recalled but which also pursued me to my construction sites in Amazonia and Indochina, without a tear. The finest ornaments on the silky gown of scales, even the delicately excised holes for the mouth and eyes—all intact. But empty.

The enthusiasm with which she showed me all the places of her new life on the coast without ever mentioning the man who had, in my view, abducted her, reflected the fact that what lay behind her, what lay behind us, was irrevocably gone. Gone too were our times as pharaoh and pharaoh queen. To me they still loomed as intoxicatingly out of our years by the Great Falls as the Bandon memorial, but to Mira they were clearly only another episode, veiled in doubt as to whether they had occurred or were wishful thinking, a daydream. She contested or passed over in silence all my objections and urged me to be silent too.

Only in our conversations about our mother Jana did we follow a common thread back into the past. Mira opened mail from Jana on the screen in the lighthouse, which showed that Jana's new companion—supposedly a water warrior on the Jordan—was actually a surveyor whose maps of the river's springs were meant to facilitate peace negotiations between Jewish settlers and Palestinian olive-oil producers sponsored by changing military headquarters; he had never been a warrior.

Jana was waiting for him to come back from surveying expeditions in mined regions to her native village of stone houses on the cliffs of Cres, a Mediterranean island that had been without water for many years now. Utterly unlike the father we knew, it said in her messages to Mira, this man always returned to her with a smile and open arms.

Curiously, our mother had told Mira about her new old life on Cres and her love affair in fragmentary messages in a language—our language—that Jana had spoken fluently at the lockmaster's house, but whose written formulation in these letters read like a stranger's from far away who had only fleetingly appropriated the vocabulary of her host country. In the village where she had grown up, clinging to the craggy coast many hundreds of feet above the beach like a bird's nest, she had re-immersed herself in the familiar idiom of her childhood, in customs, words and beliefs she had neglected for so long, and had presumably begun to forget not just the terminology of the lockmaster's house but also her whole time on the banks of the White River.

Yet whatever Jana had written to my sister, it was more, far more, than was contained in the curt messages that had reached me since we said goodbye. Comparing our electronic correspondence made my mother suddenly seem no less distant and no less missing than my father.

Are you envious? Mira asked. Jealous?

I'm surprised, I said.

The stones I had hurled at the bus that tore our mother away from the Great Falls, from Bandon and our lives for ever didn't just bounce off the black glass of the coach windows—they bounced off an illusion too.

It was the fourth—no, the fifth—day after my arrival on the North Sea coast when Mira showed me the *Amber Room*. The third of the lighthouse's four inhabited storeys, lodged between my albatross room and Mira and the dyke reeve's living space, had four portholes staring out over the sea in all directions, as did my own quarters and all the other floors, but it was completely empty. The curving surface of the circular wall consisted entirely of amber—pieces the size of a fingernail, a pebble or a fist dug out of the mud and sand or hauled to the surface as golden bycatch in drag nets, polished by the waters into murky or preciously glittering crystalline gems. They had been assembled in a kind of chaotic jigsaw in this bare circular room which looked like a treasury holding nothing but empty air, bathed in the reflected light of the ocean.

The finds had been pieced together by generations of light-house keepers and, like her predecessors, Mira would bend down repeatedly during our outings and landings on wave-swept beaches and pick up more of these resin tears shed millions of years ago or toss dull jetsam back into the sand or water.

The radically altered currents and flooding of sunken coastal landscapes, Mira said, had washed a golden bonanza from the Baltic into the North Sea. Amber collectors could now find in a month or less as much as they had once uncovered from the mud in an entire year. Maybe, Mira said, this deluge was the only effective response by the natural sea that left nothing but islands rear from the water where the maritime wilderness had once been con-creted over for subway trains, tower blocks and airports; this golden amber bonanza was therefore something like an outpouring of relief or joy.

Whenever Mira bent down for a nugget of amber, my mind went back to the fossilized oysters, isopods and prehistoric worms we had occasionally found on the sandbanks of the White River and traded for digital gaming programs with the strawberry pickers in Bandon. In this light, Mira's amber seemed like a transformation, indeed a gilding of our stones—and that made me mad.

Many of the amber fragments pieced together in the lighthouse contained organic inclusions—40, 50, 100 million-year-old bees, spiders and lacewings caught unawares in one casual and yet final movement of their lives by a droplet or trickle of tree resin and encased in it so immaculately for a form of eternity that, even 100 million years later, a dragonfly looked as if it might fly away as it was being watched and pounce on some equally ancient prey.

This circular, gold, petrified cloud which Mira walked through each time she climbed up to her living and sleeping quarters made this ascent seem like a forbidden path to heaven—or at least to me it did. The bed—be damned!—where she surely spent endless nights with her lover upon his return from the frontline of some water war, floated on a golden cloud!

During those days, Mira had never invited me—her brother and thus a guest above all suspicion—up to these heights. Tormented by hope, I had waited in vain for an invitation. If a pharaoh and a pharaoh queen still rested millennia after their deaths in caverns by the Nile, engraved with precious scrolls, and in pyramids, side by side for ever more, then why should a couple bound by blood not share the present at least, until death—and only death—parted them?

It was on the eve of my departure, which was marked on my travel permits and epidemic papers as if etched in stone, that I sought to follow my pharaoh queen through the amber cloud into the heavens without a word and without asking her permission.

I don't know if she actually noticed that I was only five or six stone steps behind her, our feet soundless as we climbed, but with every step I became increasingly certain that she not only sensed my presence as she flitted upwards with the practised grace and nimbleness of a creature made of glass, but that she would await me somewhere up above, high above, in a sphere of bliss. I was overcome by a similar all-embracing fever, like the time she had burst out of the White River in a cloud of spray and come towards me.

But when we reached the floor with the amber room and, whatever the heavens might look like, they lay still untouchably high above us, she turned to me in surprise and shock, but all she said was: *You know where your bed is. Good night.*

It was one of those long northern summer evenings when the sun had already sunk below the horizon out at sea, but the swell continued to reflect so much light into the sky that the amber room and its archaic fossils sparkled like a pyramid's burial chamber. Those tropical sites on the Mekong and the Amazon where I had dreamt of Mira—only dreamt—would already have been cloaked in darkness at that hour. However, the steel spider that would ensnare me the next morning was already stretching out its predatory arms towards me.

Before Mira could even turn away and leave me behind to continue her ascent into those upper spheres I had never seen, I had reached her and taken her in my arms. Her first, silent attempt to break free made my pincering arms automatically close more tightly, like a mechanism, a trap. Only now did I hear her voice deep down in the roar of water in my head. She was screaming. *Let go! No. Get lost!*

Numbed by the whitewater, I not only wanted to mollify my outraged sister, had to mollify my outraged sister, but had to convert her, show her that even with our different hearts we craved this thing that was happening. I pulled her, pressed her more and more tightly to me, smelt the scent of her cheeks and hair and felt the temperature of her skin. Had we not been so inseparably linked since our years in the lockmaster's house as in the gold-coated chamber of our pyramid, whose entrances had been sealed with seamless layers of granite blocks?

Let go! Get lost!

Her attempt to escape my grip was no less frantic or possessed than my attempt to hold onto her.

Let go of me, you pig!

She braced both hands against my chest, threw her head far back and leant far, far back in the trap of my embrace.

When, after a stretch of time I can no longer properly gauge and which is nonetheless chiselled into my memory, she suddenly relented in this knot of opposing forces as if she had suffered a fatal impact, lying there in my arms with her torso arching away from mine, I was sure that now at last, after so many weeks and months of longing, desire and lust, I was one with my pharaoh queen.

But then, with every beat of my pulse, she grew heavier. Now it was I who yielded and lowered her on to the bare floor flooded with amber light. How incredibly quiet it was. Not a breath could be heard from her, no exhalation, and then there was no movement or heartbeat. An expression of pain had not disfigured but estranged her face to such an extent that I whispered her name, screamed it and then whispered it again in the hope of summoning back the familiar traits to the countenance of this stranger. Her eyes remained shut, her mouth slightly open as if to utter a word I had never heard before.

What seemed to me at the time, despite my horror, to be simply Mira's fainting or, more reassuringly, a feigned bout of paralysis to fend off and halt my advances, began, like the darkness at the fall of night, only gradually to darken the amber room and reveal itself as what it truly was—death.

However, from the first instant it did not require any particular familiarity with this delicate body, whose temperature dropped lower and lower with each heartbeat of mine, to recognize that one of my glass girl's brittle cervical vertebrae must have broken in my embrace and my desperate attempt to keep my pharaoh queen in my life.

Killing my sister was such an intolerable thought that in my dreams I have groped ever since for fresh and untested terms that might banish this one word—*killing*—from my mind.

Instead of protecting my pharaoh queen and carrying her back from the sea to the White River, I have cast her out of life for the rest of time. And for what remains of mine, I will be without her—for longer, endlessly longer than a lacewing is imprisoned in a piece of amber.

NINE

Away from the Atlantic

That day, darkness rose out of the Atlantic at a speed that is usual only over rainforests and clear-cut deserts in the tropics and closed to blackness at the zenith. Not a single star was to be seen, none of the glimmering planets, not one giant sun that had shrunk to a dazzling dot millions of light years away in the boundless blackness, not one heavenly light.

No one could have said with certainty whether the firmament had been merely obscured by fog, cirrostratus or weather fronts— or had been snuffed out. And with the stars, Mira's face too had been snuffed out.

I had tried everything that came to my horrified mind to bring her back to life. To bring her back to me. I had tried with pointless caution to jolt her heart back into its old rhythm by pressing on her sternum with both hands, over and over again, but I was paralysed by the fear of shattering another piece of glass inside her, paralysed by the intuition that none of the force I deployed could reach her heart now. As I frantically tried with all my might to start her heartbeat again, should I have broken two or more ribs in her dainty, cooling body?

I had pressed my lips to hers and panted breaths into her lifeless form until I realized that I wasn't resuscitating her but kissing her. So, burning with shame, I abandoned my exertions and crouched motionlessly beside my motionless beloved who seemed to be encased in amber.

For how long? I can't remember. The tower, which began to beam out dazzling light in all directions from the glass pavilion at its summit, contained on every floor only darkness.

At some stage, like one of those robots that performs perilous tasks under water or at vertiginous heights on dams or unstable dykes, I began to prepare a bed for Mira on the bottom step of the flight of stairs leading up to her living area. Lifting up this cocoon of crystalline glass, I carried her, since pulling her body even a single yard, dragging it, would have been a fresh assault on her.

I laid her corpse, wrapped in darkness, in a position that a body could only achieve following an accidental fall and rested her head on the stone pillow of the first step. Yes, this was exactly how a person suffering from brittle bone disease would lie if she had tripped and fallen on her way up to bed and grasped in vain for the steel banister rail as she tumbled down.

Propping her head on that stone pillow in a pose congruous with such an accident, I felt the track of a tear on her cheek. Or was it my own tears I felt?

Mira, I said. Mira.

Then I slunk off into the depths. Down the spiral staircase that espoused the curve of the tower, from the extinguished gold of the amber into the darkness, a weeping, wailing creature, past the door-way to my albatross room, crawling down on all fours to the console dotted with control lamps on the ground floor. There, blazing crimson, the biggest in the multicoloured row of signals, was a fist-sized button Mira had pointed out to me as the unmistakable switch hooked up to all the back-up systems, for use in an emergency.

It was as if my punching this red glass button had unleashed the foaming waves I had not noticed until then after a long stoppage, and all of a sudden, the thunder of the sea was audible once more. Loud. Deafeningly loud. And flickering in the portholes of the control room was the reflection of a chaotic series of lights. Lightning. From deep below the horizon came lightning.

No, said the helicopter pilot who had landed on the lighthouse platform within minutes of my SOS signal, accompanied by a squad of four marines in dappled blue uniforms. No, not surf, not lightning: what I had heard was the thundering of guns. Light artillery and missile launchers. The frontline of the Elbe Water War was moving closer.

What have I done, my love. What have they done to you, Mira, my dear sister, my pharaoh queen. Fighters in fancy dress are laying you on a stretcher and dangling your bagged corpse from a rescue heli-copter because only the living are allowed on the water warriors' vehicles, planes and boats. Only the living. The dead bear the seed of destruction. The dead remind them of the end of all things and must never share a space with the living, in the air, on land or on water. The dead are ballast, a pendulum on a rope. My girl, I killed you.

After completing a recovery operation as naturally as if it were a rescue drill, the helicopter beat its way noisily through the night towards a dry mainland even the spring tides couldn't reach, where an army of mercenaries had commandeered cold-storage warehouses for its casualties from the battles on the banks of the Elbe. I stayed behind.

Earlier, I had been questioned by two of the marines under ultraviolet light (presumably the latest interrogation lamps) and pressed down the ridged surface of my index finger on three screens to confirm the truth of my statements and as a sworn signature. These screens described in large letters more commonly found in a children's book the unfolding of a tragic accident, along with photos and a scale drawing of the spiral staircase, including the iron banister her hand had groped for in vain.

I had confirmed that I was the horrified brother who had heard the crash and bang of someone falling from the bottom floor of the tower, then found his sister at the bottom of this staircase and subsequently undertaken everything possible to revive her before sounding the alarm. However, only a miracle worker could have healed that broken brittle vertebra so close to her neck. Even the helicopter pilot's view was that a weeping brother's helpless life-saving attempts could not have altered her fate.

My identity had been checked earlier, as I was flying towards the dyke reeve's tower, and obviously been classified as free of suspicious incidents. In accordance with the files designating me an essential hydraulic engineer, all the alerts issued by the dyke reeve's office had endorsed my right to visit my now-deceased sister. My permits and passes were spotless.

Also, the dyke reeve's dead partner was registered as having stayed twice in a sanatorium. Time and again, she had spent several weeks convalescing from fractures to her shoulder and pelvis on the sanatorium island of Hooge, reserved for wealthy patients. (Mira had told me that Hooge was the only tidal island preserved from submergence by a bitterly contested land-reclamation scheme, because some of the country's richest patients recuperated from war wounds and other accidental injuries there.)

The two military police officers or investigators had not expressed any doubts that someone who suffered from such a rare disease as my sister could die from falling down the stairs, but I wanted to remain available at the scene of the accident until the dyke reeve arrived, probably the next morning.

After all this had been asked and told and stammered and avowed and recorded, I was left alone in a tower that had only recently been filled with life, desire and light, watching the rotor blades of the helicopter describe circles in the lightless sky, with Mira's corpse floating from its rescue winch, and disappear in a roar that quickly faded to a hum. When this hum too had died away, the roaring in my head resumed.

Now I would never be able to follow my pharaoh queen anywhere, not into the glittering interior of a pyramid, not into the palace of a necropolis on the banks of the Nile or into one of our fantasies, let alone to any place in the real world—that was my final thought before falling asleep that night, and the first one as I woke with a start shortly afterwards and sank back exhausted into an even shorter sleep.

I had curled up on the bottom step of the amber room like one of the cats in the lockmaster's house, wrapped myself in the woollen jacket Mira had been wearing when I arrived and laid my head on the spot where I had rested hers. I inhaled her scent from the red wool and did not dare go up to the top floor of the tower.

Dragged out of my slumbers by a strident signal from one of the frenzied dreams I had that night, I groped my way down through the darkness into the now-silent control room and drank the white rum the dyke reeve kept alongside other bottles on a sideboard crafted from oar blades. I fell asleep again drunk, woke up, fell asleep and woke up until at first light I put an end to the torment of being constantly torn from dreams or unconsciousness into the realization that Mira was dead. I got up with lancing pains in my back and began to pack.

The skipper of the hovercraft that took me to the station's steel spider as one of the guaranteed connections registered on my permit, hours before the dyke reeve's planned arrival time, had heard nothing about the accident in the lighthouse nor about any injunction from the authorities. He showed me his orders, addressing me with the official title that was valid throughout the syndicate's area of operations, but he answered my enquiries about who had given him this task with the monosyllabic replies of an intimidated subordinate who would rather say nothing than get something wrong.

Inside the spider too, I passed photoelectric barriers, magnetic resonance screens and scanners on travelators reserved for hydraulic engineers and boarded the express back to Birkenau-North without once being stopped, searched or asked a single question.

In the carriage compartment accessible only to me and my colleagues, I sat down in the window seat indicated in my transit data—a registered passenger on an express that hurtled non-stop across a maze of borders towards Central Europe. But I left the train less than 10 seconds before it was sealed, having stuffed the wristband containing the details of my journey into the remote-control box of my deerskin-upholstered deckchair.

Even though the normal schedule of the North Atlantic Express would take me directly to the borders of Bandon and my new area of operations as lockmaster, should the dyke reeve or a crime agency enquire about me during this 30-hour journey, they could locate me at the press of a button and bring the train to a standstill on some heath or other, in a swamp or in the middle of dammed, flooded marshland. Like anyone else who thought they had escaped into a protective labyrinth of boundary lines on one of these express trains, I could be dragged from its sealed safety and whisked away in a speedboat, amphibious vehicle or helicopter.

And yet the tracks that had been burnt into the continent by the syndicate's surveillance systems were only a threat to those who kept to them. A hydraulic engineer, deviating no more than a hair's breadth from one of these tracks, and drawing on his knowledge of the fault lines of the continent's heaped shards and the escape routes associated with waterways, could remain invisible, at least as far as telescopic sights or infrared cameras were concerned—out of firing range and out of sight.

I was sure that Mira's blue-maned husband would not be content with records of interrogation that raised no suspicions. In even the most harmless scenario, he would ask me to account for the last hour of Mira's life. And I was equally sure that I wouldn't be able to. For although I had had to share my sister's life with this damned stranger, her death would belong to me alone. Even if I had nothing to fear from this higher-ranked favourite, there was no way I would surrender to a person who had carried my pharaoh queen away to the Atlantic.

The fragmented expanse between the North Sea and the continental interior was blocked by erratic border barriers that, like Mikado sticks or wind-strewn tree trunks, cut off almost every direct route and turned journeys into complex obstacle courses diverting travellers back to their starting point soon after they had set out or leading them into the limbo of sudden quarantine. However, a hydraulic engineer of my rank not only enjoyed privileged travel rights amid this chaotic instability, he also possessed an extensive web of maps in the memory of his navigation device—and, above all, in his head.

One of the major exams in Rotterdam had involved drawing or describing from memory watercourses, dammed areas, springs, reservoirs, the coordinates and technical infrastructure, canalization and dendritic systems of canals—in short, every water artery running above and below ground, like the paths blood takes around a many-branched organism. This web of paths—however little water the relevant trickles or rivers might be—offered a hydraulic engineer sufficient opportunities for travelling and eating. Sailors, ferrymen, lockkeepers and corrupt dam-management teams would all help him out—a shadowy community of *water folk* who derived an untraceable cash income from freshwater, whose price rose year on year, attaining astronomical levels in many arid and devastated regions, and whose only loyalty was to tax-free profiteering.

It had been demonstrated in the past that this community could even on occasions, with bribes and discreet offers, undermine the syndicate's apparent omnipotence. With this community's assistance, someone who had been cast out of the syndicate or escaped from it might become a shadow and vanish along rivers or among water meadows like a twig, a mossy stone, an otter darting across a grassy bank.

During my studies and apprenticeship in Rotterdam, and later on construction sites on the Amazon and the Mekong, I had learnt to circumvent both directives and checks in such a way that my breaches of the rules—for example, forbidden video footage of the Kayapó fighting the syndicate-backed troops on the Rio Xingu—arrows and spears against grenades and high-precision rifles—were never detected or punished. A translator working for the water-infrastructure agency in Manaus had obtained access for me to the cordoned-off battlefield near the main dam which was wreathed in smoke. In Cambodia too, I had accepted the invitation of a Khmer clan to travel incognito into Angkor's off-limits temple complexes, even though my employment contracts stated that any fraternization with tribespeople or locals would result in immediate dismissal and criminal proceedings.

Mira and I had developed a primitive code that allowed me to tell her about my excursions into illegality and the wilderness despite a host of filters on the Net. Our encryption system was so poor, however, that it repeatedly resulted in misunderstandings—for instance, until we cleared up the confusion in one of our dinner conversations in the lighthouse, Mira had actually believed that I had not witnessed a slaughter and the violent crackdown on a demonstration against the flooding of sacred hunting grounds in the Amazon but instead had attended an indió wedding featuring burnt offerings.

Mira. Even in the bulletproof-glass-and-steel waiting areas in the spider's belly, I still hoped on the morning after her death that my memories would reveal themselves to be one great, grotesque hallucination. When I nodded off, drained by this hope, and awoke startled amid the subdued bustle of a busy travel hub watched over by armed and uniformed guards, I was willing to believe each time that in the very moment of awakening, reality would turn out to be a nightmare and that the next second I would hear Mira's voice cutting through the polyphonic noise.

The shadow community wasn't a way out, but it did present me with a route. A commander on the great tidal lock visible from the spider, whom I had known when he was the coordinator of a well-building programme in a de-mining area of Cambodia, arranged a seat for me as an escort driver in a nine-truck convoy. This convoy was supposed to supply drinking water to the mansions along the Elbe after an uprising by the protectorate of Holstein against the Hamburg polity—a city-state ruled by two admirals and torn apart by near civil war.

All it had taken was an encrypted request, which I lodged from a lounge scented with lotus and lavender perfume inside the spider, to reach the commander on the tidal lock and get taken by drone to the filling station where the water transporters were gathered.

The Holsteiners . . . , said my driver, whose arms and the backs of his hands—indeed probably his whole body—were tattooed with fish heads, as the electrified-barbed-wire-lined road unfurled before his comfortable cab, the Holsteiners had tried to contaminate Hamburg's water supply with loritan, a nerve gas that blocks human blood's ability to transport oxygen within 90 seconds and can kill anyone who drinks the water. This attack had only succeeded in one upmarket residential district. He said that the tower blocks beyond the banks of the Elbe had been unaffected by a gun battle claiming many lives.

For a moment it seemed as if the driver was keen to show his happiness at this partial success. However, since he couldn't be certain that a waterman and friend of the sluice-gate commander's, a passenger entrusted to him without any explanation, was not himself a resident of this exclusive district, he merely commented: *Terrible. Everyone, even chained dogs, died with their mouths open.* He did not say another word for the remainder of the three-hour drive.

It was only as we were passing through Hamburg's border defences after nightfall—minefields, tangles of barbed wire, spring guns, and bunkers behind whose slits guards were presumably observing us through night-vision binoculars—that the driver rediscovered his tongue: *Still burning! They're still burning!*

The sky had been pale pink, as on a summer's eve, but then it flickered red, ruby red. Seven of the largest cranes in Hamburg's port (reportedly governed by an alliance of trigger-happy Friesians that had shrunk to a local faction)—rotating towers over 600 feet high with swing jibs that could have lifted a cathedral from one bank to the other—were ablaze. These towers were quite literally capable of moving mountains, as they erased hundreds of thousands of tonnes of stone and rocks and explosive material from the Canary Islands after the syndicates had strip-mined them from quarries. The islands' ravaged volcanic mountains were used for land reclamation along the mainland's sinking coastline. Compared to the gigantic stone ships, whose tonnages I remembered from calculations we had practised during my studies, even the greatest oil tankers of the past were like punts on a pond of water lilies. What a fire it was!

The driver said that the Holstein rebels had used a fleet of drones to spray thick clouds of fuel laced with an adhesive agent onto these cranes two days ago. Within minutes, these clouds had stuck to the trusses of the cranes like honey before congealing into a silvery, steel-like coating and then spontaneously combusting.

Seven inextinguishable flaming torches had transformed the sky above the port and large sections of the city into a red-hot dome. According to a message that the attackers had broadcast on the Net, this beacon, the driver said, was meant to show the land robbers of Hamburg with their trading companies, banks and marinas that democratic Holstein would never surrender to the Hanseatic city.

Cold sweat was trickling down my brow and my cheeks. I began to shake so violently that I managed to slosh a stream of water from the bottle I had just opened over the truck's dashboard. The driver didn't notice any of this. He was no less mesmerized than I was by the giant flaming torches setting the sky ablaze for the two days since the water convoy's departure. This, or something similar, is how the firmament would look during the apocalypse.

It was as if a reflection of my deed had reached me only now, with the same delay with which a thunderclap follows the lightning of a gathering storm, and I felt that it was not the dull glimmer of the amber room in Mira's tower that illuminated my deed and presented it to the eyes of the world, but these giant flares: I had killed my sister, my beloved. If I didn't want to suffocate, I had to get out into the dark, out into the open under the blood-red sky that my crime had set alight.

The driver didn't understand why it was here in this rain of fire that I chose to abandon the safety of the convoy whose water might, if need be, protect us from the heat and the flames. But in this countryside dotted with many brackish lakes, I had looked down from soaring viaducts when the wind was still and the light was good on the rows of houses and boulevards lining their bottoms on hydrographic excursions, and I knew the passages and obstacles. The Paul Bridge, the George Bridge and the Störtebeker Arch—I knew which route to take and where to find clandestine assistance.

My driver was at the wheel of the front truck, and therefore the entire convoy was forced to stop as I climbed down from the cab into the shimmering mud and was left alone in the darkness.

If there were some place on the continent, in whichever land or county it might be, that had offered my father refuge until now, that was my destination. That was where I was headed, that was where I had to go.

One sound now stood out over the thunder of water inside my head—the whirring of hummingbirds on the Rio Xingu. The air at dawn and dusk had reverberated with this whirring when four, five or even six different species of hummingbirds had sipped sugared water from the glass flutes decorated with plastic flowers that used to sway in the wind on my terrace. The sound of their blood-red and emerald-green wings could not be drowned out by the water or the wind, the noise of distant engines or the polyphonic chorus coming from the rainforest. In this rhythmic whirr I thought I detected syllables that combined to state a mission, an order that I was to carry out after my father's crime at the Great Falls and the deaths of five people in his care: *Kill him! Kill him!*

Kill him. After Amazonia, even the kingfishers on the Mekong would shower me with these three syllables as they plunged from low-hanging branches into the water in pursuit of their prey—fish illuminated by the afternoon sun as they drifted in the shallow water, crabs that ventured into the current in slow motion and ended up in a kingfisher's beak on a bank where only those with lungs could breathe and where their shells would be smashed and their sweet flesh devoured.

However, in the glow of the flaming harbour cranes, these syllables, whipped up by birds' wings from a sediment of dark dreams, memories and angry fantasies from somewhere deep inside me, began to disperse. They gave way to a new name, a more urgent quest. Two syllables: Jana. My mother's name stood out with complete clarity, just as words, phrases or orders leap out so clearly from a chaotic hubbub of voices that they seem to have been pronounced against a backdrop of silence, deathly silence.

And this clarity had brought home to me, even before I had abandoned the protection of the water convoy, that one path must take precedence over all other paths of retribution or rage and take me southwards to the Adriatic Sea. Now that I had killed someone—my dearest love, my sister—I was overcome that evening when the sky appeared to be on fire by the same immense longing for comfort and reassurance as I had felt when I once cut up wasps and hornets in mid-air by the Great Falls and then burst into tears in disgust at my act, at the sight of their severed bodies in the moss or on the stones.

Afterwards, in Jana's arms, I had discovered how comforting the warmth and scent of her skin could be and how soothing the gentle pressure of her embrace. A crime and despair at my own cruelty could even be lightened in Jana's arms, as later in Mira's arms, and evaporate like the spectres of a nightmare in the instant of waking.

Jana. I had to go to her. Go to her and give her my account of Mira's death. As the only witness to a tragic accident, I would swear that I wasn't what I truly was—a killer—and in this way I would take the sting out of reality. I would talk, talk and tell her what had happened until an ordeal that could only be endured as a story would be transformed into a story, into words. And Jana would console me for the death of my pharaoh queen, which threatened to plunge me into despair. My destination was Jana's island. The island of her birth, Cres, which had been conquered by a Venetian triumvirate the previous year and once more bore an Italian name: Cherso.

It was strange how calming I found the thought of following my lost mother to her island devastated by the Dalmatian wars and deprived of water by bombing and the poisoning of its springs and wells. If the direct route to the Mediterranean through the middle of a shattered continent was blocked by border checkpoints, then I would follow the rhizomes of rivers, streams and canals flowing down from its main watershed to the coastline where the city of Rijeka had defended itself in vain. After the Venetians had taken control, Rijeka's ruins too had been forced to adopt their old name of Fiume.

Regardless of these newly baptized lands, I knew the manager of a fishing cooperative controlled by the syndicate whose drag-net trawlers could carry me over to Jana's island. Venetians or Dalmatians: the syndicate cultivated relations with rulers old and new. In the running battles that regularly flared up around dams, tribal areas, coastlines and riverbanks, the victor of yesterday could swiftly become the vassal of tomorrow.

However, if a hydraulic engineer like me knew how to make use of the knowledge he had acquired in Rotterdam and his freedom of movement in this labyrinth of nationalist fanatics and fragmented network of new factions of water junkies, and if he could put his pursuers off his scent by building baffling deviations into his route, carry no electronic location devices in his baggage or on his body and occasionally lie low for a few days, then even a killer, a murderer who had killed the only person he loved in the whole world, could go wherever he wanted like a free man.

TEN

Through a Shattered World

As well as endless columns of water-level marks, current speeds, pressure conditions and the cubic contents of freight cargo, the storage modules from the computer in the lockmaster's house contained audio recordings of over two dozen messages from a preacher our father had clearly revered as a prophet. After the lockmaster's house had been cleared—and before the modules were confiscated by the syndicate—Mira had once sent these sermons, performed alternately in a whisper, a roar or a song, along with many years of archived measurements of the White River, in encrypted form to me in Amazonia: *Father's Howler Monkey*.

Mountains and plains, entire continents even . . . these were the words I heard the preacher—who called himself *Acheron* after the mythical river that emptied into the Ionian Sea—proclaiming through the earpieces of my headphones, interrupted by occasional cries, bursts of coughing and applause from his congregation . . . Mountains and plains, he said, were thrust upwards by the forces of erosion, volcanic activity or displacement of the Earth's crust into the icy clouds and then, over the course of many millions of years, sank back into the deep.

Europe, Asia, America, Australia, Greenland and other parts of the Earth with short-lived names drifted apart like rafts during this process, shattered or fused by disasters spanning many more millions of years—beneath a starry sky that was no less temporary and was strewn in infinite particles of dust—into new supercontinents, or were consumed in volcanic fireworks. The ashes accumulated in front of mountains of tectonic rubble or were dashed against beaches of sand and shingle. Viewed in fast forward, however, these seemingly immortal coastlines were just a ribbon slapping in the wind and fluttering through the ages.

But, the preacher shouted, that which hardened into dry land, reared up or spread out in all directions and burst apart, was subject to the laws of gravity, and the forces of division would sooner or later tear it apart in every dimension of space—from the intergalactic to the most minute battlegrounds of matter on a scale only quantum physicists could measure.

Yet if the highest mountain ranges reverted to dust and trickling sand, the final state of any landscape, even the most powerful empire was destined to crack into ever-smaller fragments, into regions, city-states, tribal areas, clans and indeed families—and ultimately into a host of individuals.

The North American and European continents, bound together for centuries by a shared history of cruelty, conquest, slavery and genocide, had long been on the path towards a more peaceful future, the preacher yelled—no, sang—over the unrest in a hall or some rallying place. On the path to a more peaceful future! For eventually only scattered bands of the thirst-stricken would come to blows over a cup of murky freshwater, and a few hungry people over a scrap of meat, but they could no longer wage wars . . . The preacher left a long pause before a chorus of *Amen! Amen!* was heard.

No more wars! For if one day everyone was fighting everyone else for a stony strip of land a hand's breath above the waters, the age of armies, battlefields and bombed-out cities would finally be over. *Amen!*

None of what filtered through the headphones at deafening volume was new to me—these *sand clerics* and *water priests*, admonishers and visionaries with all kinds of predictions about the future of mankind had been a daily occurrence on screens and in spiritual sites filmed by dozens of cameras during my school days—but this recording of Mira's was the first time I had heard that our father was an acolyte or perhaps even an *illuminatus*.

The copy from the lockmaster's house, which was now stored on a magnet-proof segment of my data wrist strap, which could be hooked up wirelessly to a screen, also revealed correspondence between my father and the syndicate and his futile attempts to avert Jana's deportation back to her Mediterranean homeland. His petitions to the migration office in Bandon contained dozens of long documents—answers, appeals, objections—and repeated professions of his love for his wife, each and every word of them as fresh and unprecedented as if they had come from another planet.

Confronted with the overwhelming abundance of this material, I was struck by a thought that had hitherto appeared outlandish to me. My father had found in Jana not just a maid, a consoler, an assistant for managing the Great Falls and the mother of his two children, doubtless also a source of financial benefits as part of a demographic development scheme; he had also found a lover. The grim, taciturn lockmaster had loved Jana.

Whether Mira had meant these files as evidence of this love or simply wanted to share with me the visions of our father's guru-preacher, will for ever remain a mystery.

I listened to this material during a sleepless night in a surge chamber, crisscrossed with pipelines, belonging to the Hamburg flood authorities. I had been allowed to wait there, from where the local suspension railway to the Kingdom of Hanover left the next morning. This time it was a mineral-water trader who had arranged for me to travel another stage undetected by surveillance networks.

The Hanoverians were highly indebted to the syndicate for the construction of a dyke, a huge bulwark almost 60 miles long that was intended to preserve their embattled monarchy from collapse. Any representative of this almighty creditor organization therefore only needed to prove his affiliation to the syndicate by having his iris scanned at one of their optical barriers to use any of the transport infrastructure within the kingdom's network—suspension railways, ferries, hydrogen buses—without charge and without passport checks.

The next morning, when I entered the luxury compartment of the Mediterranean-bound suspension railway, fitted with armchairs and aquariums teeming with brightly coloured ornamental fish, I was paralysed by the idea that I was embarking on a journey through the preacher's visions. Ahead of me lay a jigsaw of fanatical microstates, the shards of a continent where the anthem, the flag, the coat of arms, the currency and the colour of the border posts changed every 20 to 30 miles—entities united only by their wretchedness. Any part of this fragmented world that lacked precious commodities such as mineral-rich freshwater, metals, salts for the Asian electronics industries or at least a skilled technical workforce had no choice but to live off the fruits of its fields and gardens and replace every worn-down component of its rattling broken machines with human labour.

With every additional declaration of independence, the pan-continental patchwork that my father's preacher had invoked to his congregation as a divinely ordained step on the way to a more peaceful personal future lost another name that might remind people of the old Europe. By the time I went to school in Bandon, Europe was just the name of a Phoenician king's mythical daughter kidnapped and raped by a horny god, not a name capable of gluing random fragments together.

After stepping off the royal suspension railway at a terminus overgrown with ivy and Virginia creepers, I struck out for the sea on a journey that resembled the advances and knight moves of a piece in a board game, zigzagging between strips of no man's land, restricted areas, minefields, quarantine zones and sovereign territories surrounded by layers of electric fencing, most of which were so ridiculously small than even a bird no faster than a rock pigeon could have flown across them in a hour. And in front of each one, above it, behind it, stood a dense forest of electronic or steel barriers.

Despite having been trained to infiltrate any territory unde-tected, never before had I actually been forced to exercise this skill on a daily basis and not in jest.

Now, though, my route would lead me across the shattered continent with all its unstable alliances, barriers and technical sur-veillance systems of varying degrees of sophistication. Working to my advantage was the fact that the only systems that genuinely spanned the individual regions and microstates were the syndicate's own networks. The power of local security forces, checkpoints and armies ended at the nearest border crossing. None of them exchanged information with their neighbour because, in times like these, every neighbour was considered an enemy. Someone acquainted with the syndicate's eyes and ears had no reason to fear local law enforcement.

I cannot remember how many days passed as I hopped across this checkerboard, yearning for someone to comfort me. At some stage, I had to admit to myself that, again and again, despite the burden of my crime, I was enjoying the irreversible nature of my journey to the sea, meandering like a river current striving towards its estuary.

I often travelled across country, led only by the digital voices and instructions of my navigator, along and over forest boundaries, swimming across border rivers with my meagre luggage packed into water-tight bags, following the course of streams and water-ways whose sources and mouths I could have reeled off in my sleep. Occasionally I made use of transport options old friends in the syndicate organized for me by satellite communications—for instance, convoys of trucks carrying stone, a few times even drones and small aircraft that flew under the syndicate's radar.

On the heavy-metal-contaminated Magdalena River, which had swollen over the past decade to a width of almost 20 miles, the pilot of a jetfoil offered to take me across for a fraction of the normal price of passage. After a breakneck crossing, which soaked both of us and even my supposedly waterproof luggage, he asked me if I wanted to buy some weapons—hand grenades, flame-throwers, automatic rifles. When I reacted to this offer at first as if it was a bad joke and then turned it down flat, he flew into such a fury that he threatened me with a flick knife and only left me alone when I shouted out the name of a friend who commanded a militia on this stretch of the river.

From then on, I only used river ferries, some of them vintage steamers flying the insignia of a local warlord, to cross lakes that had flooded to many times their original size. Scouts from rebel minorities guided me over deforested mountain chains, and I crossed the border into Greater Serbia in a caravan of travelling labourers escorted by robots. But nothing I saw or heard during my travels could drown out the incessant roar of water inside my head nor Mira's voice, embedded there as if in a cocoon. Whispering familiar pet names to me, laughing at me, giving warnings and commands, sometimes mimicking our father's voice.

Next, I would be dozing and daydreaming in the back of a pickup or a van packed with skeletal pickers from harvest camps, and I hoped that all these experiences and everything I thought I knew about the state of the continent was based on a similar misunderstanding to Mira's assumption that I had merely been a guest or a witness at an indió wedding rather than a massacre . . .

But these fantasies quickly faded due to the hardships of my journey and gradually dwindled as I approached the coast of the Adriatic. The blueness and the islands of this adjacent sea, more like a lake than an ocean when compared with the size of the Pacific or the Atlantic, had appeared to me as the location of boundless adventures during my school days in Bandon, as the greatest source of myths and other forms of culture too. The idea that there might be other seas along whose shores perhaps even greater civilizations had flourished (before being destroyed or enslaved by Mediterranean powers) had for many years struck me as the slanderous chatter of charlatans.

Was it not the wealthy Egyptians, Phoenicians, Assyrians, Greeks, Romans, Umayyads and Ottomans who had initiated a grandeur that had not been surpassed for millennia—even though ultimately, according to the teachings of the preacher whose voice my father had saved in the modules in the lockmaster's house, this grandeur was always destined to crumble back into the fragmented wasteland I had to cross on my way to Jana.

What a morning, what a moment when I spied the seemingly placid blue of the sea of heroes from a ridge in Istrian no man's land, encaged by the trunks of a light pine forest. This blueness had carried the ships of Odysseus and Agamemnon; and this blueness had been reflected in the eyes of Helen and Penelope and Nausicaa, that melancholy king's daughter. The pharaohs' captains had hoisted their drag anchors nearly five thousand years ago before the harbour walls of Rhacotis and, after many months of wandering, brought back news across this blueness to their all-powerful ruler that the world was larger than any imperial dream the pharaohs might immortalize with pyramids.

The island that lay before me that morning far below in the Bay of Fiume, its foaming waves like drifting snow, was familiar from a mouldy watercolour on the wall in the lockmaster's house that my mother Jana had cherished like an icon yet left behind. Perhaps she had left it behind in the hope that Mira and I might at least have some notion, however washed-out the painting was, of where our mother had disappeared to. *Cherso*, or, as it known before its conquest by a Venetian fleet: *Cres*.

The Dalmatian wars had so devastated and depopulated the island that there was no sign of life on the long, stony, landward coast of Cherso as I spent many futile hours roaming the alleyways of Fiume, enquiring about a ferry. That night, which I spent in a hostel where the crews of water tankers and boring ships waited for their assignments, the only light on Cherso was the dull winking of automatic sea marks.

The navigator of a boring ship, who was due to set out the next day in search of undersea springs of fresh water, had made it his life's goal to ascend into the caste of hydraulic engineers, and he spoke to me in the hostel's news lounge in the belief that I might potentially act as his advocate. After four or five cocktails at a bar whose surface flickered with mercurial images, he sent me his contact details and had no suspicions when I did not recip-rocate, citing security guidelines.

The next morning, on what was forecast to be a boiling-hot autumn day, one of the boring ship's dinghies dropped me off at the quay of an abandoned village on Cherso's rocky north coast. The quay and the surrounding cliffs were so overgrown with thorny bushes that the navigator lobbed me a foot-long boat knife from the dinghy, without which my landing would have been like advancing through barbed-wire defences.

During the crossing, the navigator had warned me of the mountain path I would have to take if I planned to reach Montalto, the only remaining inhabited village, Jana's village, that day. Cherso, he said, had been transformed during the Dalmatians wars from an Adriatic idyll into a kind of antechamber of hell, its villages burnt to the ground, its wells and cisterns filled in, and an entire lake, the island's freshwater reservoir poisoned, if not for ever, then for a century at least. On this tiny, miserable bit of land, you might even die of thirst or in a fight for a canister of drinking water, if desperation did not drive you to save yourself by swimming across the strait teeming with stinging algae and recently arrived biting eels from Cherso to the Istrian peninsula and its water reserves. And even if you did pull off this feat, there was a serious risk of wading up the beach into sniper fire because the Venetians were still battling partisan resistance fighters there and, out of fear of their enemies' mercilessness and implacable patriotism, shot anyone who didn't identify themselves as a Venetian subject quickly enough first and asked questions later.

I laboured under my full water-rucksack which I had acquired from the boring ship's equipment stores in return for a promise that I would file a grateful report to the syndicate about the crew's assistance.

The ship had already disappeared behind a spit of land when I scrambled through the ruins of a coastal village and came across a forest of strawberry trees and, at long last, tracks leading up into the hills. It was strange to have a satellite-assisted electronic navigation device at my disposal, which could determine my position down to a matter of inches, and yet still have to blaze a trail through the wilderness in the same way as people had done for hundreds of years. With an axe. With a knife.

The lines indicating altitude and incline on my pathfinder screen had suggested a moderate ascent, but without my knife I could not have penetrated the pricking, stinging thicket that covered the slopes here, complete with mantraps, loitering nooses and thorns. I could not walk. I could not climb. I crawled.

It was as if the Dalmatian wars had cast a web over this island that eradicated only human life and afforded wildlife, especially insects, new opportunities to thrive.

By the time dusk came and I had climbed the first of three ridges separating me from Montalto, I was studded with bruises and the glowing marks of insect stings and mosquito and horsefly bites like a scarlet-fever sufferer, and I had to remind myself and even shout at myself not to cool the burning red rash with my drinking water.

Until the floods triggered by melting glaciers at the end of the last ice age, Cherso had been the tip of a mountain range bound to the mainland by fertile valleys, and only when the continent warmed up did it become part of a wave-beaten archipelago including many other mountains and ridges. With the ongoing and unstoppable rise in sea level, this island would revert to being an underwater mountain, on whose cliffs and rocky flanks shoals of fish pursued by dolphins would cast their shadows.

It was impossible to reach Montalto that day. The overgrown carters' tracks and roads I occasionally crossed that petered out into brush or were cut off by shell holes or scree slopes offered no prospect of a waggon or, at the very least, a rider. Motorized vehicles, the navigator had told me, had long since vanished from the islands in the upper reaches of the Adriatic. This coastal region, poor in raw materials and freshwater, was just a buffer zone now, a battlefield.

I spread some parched grass over a carpet of lichen on the future sea floor. Despite their frugal needs, the copper-coloured lichens had dried out years ago—just one more sign that the levels of precipitation in this region of the Mediterranean Sea had dwindled to those of the southern Sahara. People without access to water here either had to fight for it or die.

On construction projects in Amazonia, Laos and Cambodia, I had often slept outside and allowed myself to be lulled to sleep by the ceaseless choruses of wildlife. Here, though, it was as silent as in a sandy desert. Even the stinging, biting, sucking insects carried out their raids on my sweat-soaked body soundlessly. It may have been, however, that the whirring of their wings was simply drowned out by the roaring noise inside my head, which was more deafening in this quietness than all the water of the Great Falls.

ELEVEN

Forgiveness

At the end of a night spent half-asleep between periods of confused alertness, I did after all sprinkle my swollen eyelids and lachrymal sacs with some water to soothe the fire. Mosquitoes, shimmering bluebottles and horseflies had attacked me in numbers and with a ferocity I had only ever experienced in the tropics. However, Montalto, my navigation device said, was no more than a seven hours' walk away, even at the crawling pace of my progress so far. I would be able to cope with that distance through thickets and landslides without slaking my thirst, and so it was all right to cool my glowing skin with precious water from the boring ship's tanks until I reached my destination.

For the first hour after I struck out, a screeching flock of herring gulls accompanied me in a peculiar, spiralling flight, as if they hoped that I would lead them to abundant hunting grounds, a bay amid this now fish-free sea that was whipped to a frenzy by beating fins. Yet when the flock took their leave on a ridge that was covered with dead holm oaks as suddenly as they had initially whirled around me, I realized that it had not been me leading the seabirds, but the swarm of gulls guiding me.

Far below me, bordered by scree slopes and singed maquis, lay the lake Jana had described to us so often by the White River that, without having ever seen even a video of its glittering dark-blue surface, my sister and I felt we knew it as intimately as the pools and gravel banks of the White River and its banks overflowing with orange lilies and wild orchids.

Like the setting of one of Jana's stories brought to life, the lake lay there in the morning sun, as beautiful as in the fairy tales she used to tell us: Crow Lake, the last remnant of ice-age flooding and for centuries the only drinking-water reservoir for the islands of Cherso and Lussin, which had once been linked by a now-wrecked swing bridge. The shores of this wonder had long been stripped of all life, however. The First Dalmatian War had poisoned every drop of this lake for generations and made it lethal even for the most primitive forms of life. Anyone who bathed in this water or drank it, I had been informed on the boring ship, would be unable to reach Montalto or the quayside via which they had stepped ashore on this cursed island.

The lake bottom, Jana had told us, dropped down abruptly from the floor of the high valley, in which it was contained like a trough, to far below the surface of the sea, which is why people in her village had recounted anecdotes about glowing molluscs, jellyfish and other denizens of the deep floating along the dark lake bottom while trout, bream, pike and other freshwater fish splashed about in the upper layers of water nearer the sun.

According to the legend which Mira and I regularly entreated Jana to tell us, there were not only glowing alien life forms living at the bottom of the lake; on the night of the first full moon of every year, chants of repentance would rise up from a sunken cathedral that had been submerged along with its builders during one hundred years of rains.

With these floods, a long-forgotten pagan goddess had punished this town and its inhabitants, amassers of great fortunes from the slave trade, for their cruelty and their greed and also for their crimes against birdlife. The sinners used to keep songbirds in cages and drew pleasure and joy from them during the winter months before killing them in the spring and frying their tongues over the embers of Easter fires as a delicacy; they trained hawks and falcons and poisoned crows to protect their lakeside hanging gardens from the hungry scavengers. The word for crow in Jana's mother tongue was *Vrana*, hence the name of the lake.

From Crow Lake, the elongated shadows on its surface ruffled by a light breeze, the thermals wafted up to me a bitter, metallic aroma. This body of water, cursed by a goddess and poisoned with biological weapons, had stayed with me from Jana's storytelling until my geology lectures in Rotterdam. There, Lake Vrana had been presented as a perfect example of a *cryptodepression*, a water-filled hollow surrounded by the Adriatic. The lake's shoreline lay far above sea level, its bottom far below it, though. Cherso had been presented as an example of the precious nature of such geological phenomena—a freshwater lake in the middle of a sea!

It was strange to stand in this shadeless landscape and, in the centre of a vast panorama, see the backdrop of Jana's fairy tales as scenes from real life. Until this moment I had known Crow Lake only from Jana's descriptions and from screens and graphic displays on wallcharts in Rotterdam, and yet this sight seemed no less real than any of my memories from the Great Falls.

After the flock of gulls had dispersed, it became so quiet that even the flapping wings of tiny, pale moths were audible as they lifted off from the ashes of lichen and moss under my feet. And in the heart of this quietness, I realized with sudden shock that the incessant roar that had dominated the inside of my head for so long had subsided. Within me and around me it was, apart from the pounding of my blood in my ear canals, completely silent.

The very next moment I was convinced that this silence must have coincided with the sight of a skyline atop the mountain ridge high above me, like rows of teeth jutting from the jaw of a fossilized predatory fish: steep-pitched, crushed roofs, shattered walls, a bell-tower—every building a petrified tooth in the mouth of a mega-lodon that had perished 15 or 20 million years ago on the peaks of a submarine mountain range. A village completely built of stone the same lead-grey colour as the surrounding rocks: Montalto. Jana had set out from here with the hope of a more positive life. And she had come back here.

According to the shading of the contour lines my navigator displayed, Montalto stood on a craggy ridge running from east to west and falling away abruptly and sometimes vertically to the north, vertically to the south—down in cascades of stone, over 1,000 feet down to the sea.

As if some magical force were seeking to prevent me from reaching the village's collapsed defensive walls, even desiccated, leafless thorn bushes thickened into impassable obstacles. As I toiled uphill, step by step, one time along the supposedly easier route of a dry, stony stream bed, down which long-vanished cloud-bursts had sent torrents pouring towards the contaminated Crow Lake, the village above me took on the form and structure of the rocks to such a degree that its buildings gradually gave the impression that they had been carved into or broken from the hillside thousands of years ago but repeatedly subsumed back into the mountain.

There were no recognizable roads or tracks leading up to the huddled stone houses from whose burst walls the branches of tamarisks and mulberry trees waved at me. Montalto had obviously turned its back on the island's devastated northern slopes, from a poisoned lake and the haze-veiled mainland, but also on the entire fractured continent, peering out of gaping windows at the sea and nothing else.

However, when I finally reached the padlocked portal of the belltower at the entrance to the village after one final excruciating ascent, I saw five or six houses whose slate roofs glinted in the sunlight as if newly done, as if life had crawled out of the depths of the sea and over the southern rockfaces into the ruins, eager to make a fresh start in the midst of this solitude.

My arms and legs were covered in scratches and insect bites, and I struggled to fend off the swarms of flies driven mad by the congealed trickles of blood. I washed off the blood with the last drops from my reserves. The tempting sound of water was audible in the cistern next to the belltower. Perhaps the cistern was actually fed by a live spring.

Yet despite the long ladle lying beside a cast-iron manhole cover decorated with an angel, this water was inaccessible, because this angel spread his wings over a shining locked iron bar. During medieval droughts, Jana had told us, Crow Lake had become as salty as the sea, and water thieves were pushed off a rocky outcrop on the edge of the village into the void.

For over four thousand years, I had read on my data strap, people had been living here high above Crow Lake, whose water, millennia later, had turned not just salty but into a lethal brew. It was clear, however, that there were still supply routes and lifelines up to Montalto from the crescent beach below. The hairpin bends of a footpath cut into the cliffs, leading upwards from a soot-blackened beacon platform next to the reservoir, and people and beasts of burden took it to transport food and certainly water from a quay up to the hilltop village. There was no way, given the scarcity of rain at this latitude, that cisterns alone could preserve even a half-ruined village from thirst and drought. There were no visible helicopter pads. Only this winding path connecting a low-lying pebble beach via some cascading rocks with Montalto's last inhabited stone houses (or were they the first of a fresh start?). The houses with roofs clung like swallows' nests amid the overgrown ruins on the south-facing slope, whereas to the north, on the Crow Lake side, it was all ruins.

Alerted by the panicked cry of a blackbird, I suddenly thought I heard voices coming from one of the houses—but they were carried off on a hissing gust of wind. A fountain of dust whirled up from the flat roof of a stable or a barn, enveloping me for a second and burning my scratched skin. As I made to cool off the itchy spots with a handful of muddy water from a puddle, I caught sight of a piece of paper flapping on the southern wall of the bell-tower in the biting wind.

On a whitewashed board nailed to the wall, the kind of death announcements I had seen in many coastal villages—black-bordered announcements, printed with faded photos, stating which people had left their fellow citizens, which people had departed this world. Messages like this tugged at their rusting drawing pins until they faded into illegibility and the news of an individual's death looked like a watermark on a sheet of fly-specked white paper.

It was eight, seven, six steps from the muddy puddle to the death announcements, but I had already spied Mira's picture among the obituaries before I reached the board. Mira. My laughing sister. Her picture was framed by the verses of a text I could not understand—maybe a lament, maybe a prayer or perhaps merely the details of the deceased. Every word was in my mother's language. Jana had proclaimed her daughter's death to the last, or the first, returning inhabitants of Montalto.

How well I knew the picture on the whitewashed board. Our father had taken it on one of those March days when we paid a visit via a narrow sluice gangplank to a water-beaten rock below the Great Falls. When meltwater time came, deep-blue gentians and spreading primroses of such a golden yellow that to our minds as children it was not just comprehensible but indubitable when Jana called these flowers *keys to heaven*. They opened the gardens of the angels to humans.

But where were those gardens? In the spray, Jana had said, in the feathery clouds and even in the ochre-coloured tornadoes that whirled around the pharaoh columns of Bandon in the summer. The gates of these gardens, Jana had said, were as numerous as the inhabitants of the Earth, and although they would not open for each and every person, they would at least reveal themselves. Those who had a key would be able to enter paradise.

That March day, my father had called Mira's name through the thunderous noise, then eventually shouted it to get her to turn towards him and his camera for one of the many souvenir pictures he collected not in storage modules but in albums as thick as his logbooks of measurements, which he labelled with a piece of chalk.

Mira had finally looked back over her shoulder at him, laughing. She was pressing the precious flower, which Jana allowed each of us to pick each year, to her chest, invisible to the camera's eye. I knew that she had been clasping this key to heaven in her fist; we had picked our annual primrose moments earlier from the same cushion of moss.

Despite being two or three paces away from the whitewashed noticeboard, the announcement of the death of my sister, my pharaoh queen, hit me with such force that I sank to my knees, my field of vision filled with my laughing Mira. Although my body was freezing, as if I had been brushed by the cold breeze from a glacier, I felt a trickle of sweat run down my cheeks and over my chin. From there it dripped into the dust, each salty drop forming a tiny crater like the impact of a tiny meteorite speeding out of the infinity of space.

Thou shalt not kill, I heard myself whisper over and over again, like the refrain of a prayer or a comforting phrase, a magic formula. *Thou shalt not kill.*

Hadn't our lessons in Bandon explained that commandments like this were the will of a whiny god who could no longer understand or cope with the bloodthirstiness and cruelty of his own creatures, and therefore permitted cataclysmic floods to unfurl upon their cities?

And then, abruptly, the gusty wind ceased, creating a sudden bubble of silence in which I repeatedly heard that voice, a voice so soft that its message seemed to be nothing but a manifesto of tenderness.

This sound was coming from one of the flat roofs leading down like steps to the edge of the void, down to the cliffs, down to the sea, which was carrying a horizon embroidered with narrow bands of cloud.

And then, with Mira's rustling death announcement behind me, looking out towards the sea, into the fuzzy distance, I saw Jana. Standing by a collapsed wall that sloped down from the belltower to one of the roofed houses on the edge of the drop, I saw my mother. She was kneeling on the roof between cobs of corn that had been laid out to dry and was speaking to a puppy jumping up at her. I would have recognized the gentle and soothing tone of that voice among all the sounds and tones in this world.

Jana. She was trying to free the young dog's black-and-white furry coat of some burrs or thorns snagged in it, but the puppy mistook her attempts for a game and kept wriggling out of her grasp in anticipation of being caught again, held and stroked. Jana went along with this but then, speaking over the puppy's head without altering her tone of voice, addressed another creature—but whether this was an animal or a human only became clear when the addressee stepped out from the porch on the flat roof carrying a basket full of maize cobs. My father.

For the second time that day I fell to my knees, but this time not because I was overcome with emotion but because, for a few seconds, I needed to be alone in the shade and shelter of the waist-high remains of a wall with the sight that had presented itself to me on the flat roof as if on a clifftop stage high above the sea: my parents, for many years cold and estranged towards each other, as loving man and loving wife.

From my hiding place I now heard the lockmaster's voice, but I couldn't understand what reply he gave to Jana's words. He spoke as quietly as he used to in the lockmaster's house when Mira and I would eavesdrop through an unlatched door as Jana reminded him that the children were asleep. For many nights in my child-hood, this door had to remain ajar because, despite Mira's reassurance, I was scared of the dark.

Had my father staged his own drowning in order to join his wife in her homeland? In doing so, had he turned his back on the distant past, ceased to hark back to the lockmaster's lost glory and authority, and yearned for his years with Jana instead? It seemed, on the flat roof below me, as if he had arrived in the present, with Jana.

But that man bearing a basket of corn cobs, which he then laid out before this woman like an offering to an idol—was he the murderer of five people? Like a forgetful person whose mind has let slip the most familiar names over time or with the progression of a disease, I had no evidence. I could no longer remember.

During our childhood by the Great Falls, the mere tone of Jana's voice had determined what was wrong and what was good for our lives, what was likeable and what was to be feared or even fought. In all respects of our lives on the banks of the White River, Jana's judgement had been infallible. She would have had nothing more to do with a murderer, ever, even if he was the father of her children, her father, her lover or her brother. Her parting words to him would have been a curse.

When I got up from my hiding place, relieved that I had the wall for support, I saw Jana brushing a strand of hair from my father's face while the puppy leapt up at her. My parents would only have needed to turn towards my wall to see me. But they had eyes only for each other.

I saw the gutter of the flat roof as a boundary between the sunbathed rows of corn cobs, glowing the same golden-yellow colour as the keys to heaven, and the cascading rocks beyond, the edge of the abyss. In my mind I counted the footsteps that would take me over the ruined wall to the flat roof below me and to my father. No more than two, maybe three breaths, and I would have reached him and grabbed him by the shoulders and hurled him over that boundary into the void and out of this world.

A human being who crashed down onto these cascading rocks from the height of the village and then tumbled on and on from the bloodstained site of his impact would be transformed into raw meat—his skull shattered, his breaking bones jagging like daggers from skeins of muscle and layers of fat. If there were no merciful gust of wind to erase the noise of this falling and dying, then a fracturing of bones would be audible, the cracking of shinbones, hips, the top of the skull. And then silence—stunned silence at a long trail of blood zigzagging down the rocks.

But I . . . I stand by my wall and hear none of these things. See the bulging, glowing-red scar on my father's hand, the marks of the broken chain of a sluice gate. Hear only Jana's unbelievably gentle voice.

Whatever the man who now rocks her in his arms may have done to her or to the world—she has forgiven him. And if it was simply carelessness, a moment's recklessness or sheer excitement about a flamboyant spectacle in honour of a drowned saint at the Great Falls, causing the deaths of five people . . . whatever it was that potentially drove this lockmaster to the brink of despair and then eventually back to her, because only with her could he find comfort or at least a little mollification—she had forgiven him.

She had helped him to sail out of his memory-flooded world into one that was yet to be discovered, and had passed him off there as her new husband and partner—even in her messages to Mira. Even in her messages to the pharaoh queen. And she had assented to his apparent death. In doing so, she had protected him—including from his own past.

The top of the crumbling wall slides under my palm like the banister of a staircase. I begin to follow the wall, slowly, step by step, so as not to dislodge a stone and startle the couple on the flat roof. I go down, step by step, down to the place where cut stones furred with moss and lichen meet the hairpin path hewn into the cliffs.

I follow its snaking route, as imperturbable as a rivulet that first has to seek its path through scree and soil and sand and yet, guided by the gravitational force that governs all time and space, has only one goal: the sea.